I0615429

Henry William Little

One Man's Power

The Life And Work of Emin Pasha in Equatorial Africa

Henry William Little

One Man's Power
The Life And Work of Emin Pasha in Equatorial Africa

ISBN/EAN: 9783744752954

Printed in Europe, USA, Canada, Australia, Japan

Cover: Foto ©Raphael Reischuk / pixelio.de

More available books at **www.hansebooks.com**

EMIN PASHA.

(EDUARD SCHNITZER.)

From Sketch by Dr. Felkin.

ONE MAN'S POWER.

The Life and Work

OF

EMIN PASHA

IN

EQUATORIAL AFRICA

BY

THE REV. HENRY W. LITTLE

AUTHOR OF "MADAGASCAR: ITS HISTORY AND PEOPLE," "HOW TO SAVE EGYPT," ETC., ETC., ETC.

With Portrait and Map

LONDON

J. S. VIRTUE & CO., LIMITED, 26, IVY LANE

PATERNOSTER ROW

1889

LONDON:
PRINTED BY J. S. VIRTUE AND CO., LIMITED,
CITY ROAD.

PREFACE.

THE great Anglo-Saxon and English-speaking nations of the Old and New Worlds as yet have no succinct and convenient record of the life and work of Emin Pasha in Equatorial Africa.

These pages, it is hoped, will in some measure supply the need.

The narrative is based upon the Pasha's own letters, and official and original documents, for the use of which the writer is indebted to Sir Francis De Winton, K.C.M.G., C. H. Allen, Esq., F.R.G.S., and others.

The helpful lessons of such a career, so strong in purpose, so direct in aim, and so prolific in results to the future well-being of the native races of the Dark Continent, are too valuable to be overlooked or forgotten. The life of Emin Pasha is worthy of careful and attentive study, as an example of "one man's power," and as a striking illustration of the marvellous force of individuality, when directed to a single purpose, and inspired by a lofty sense of duty.

H. W. L.

LONDON, 1889.

CONTENTS.

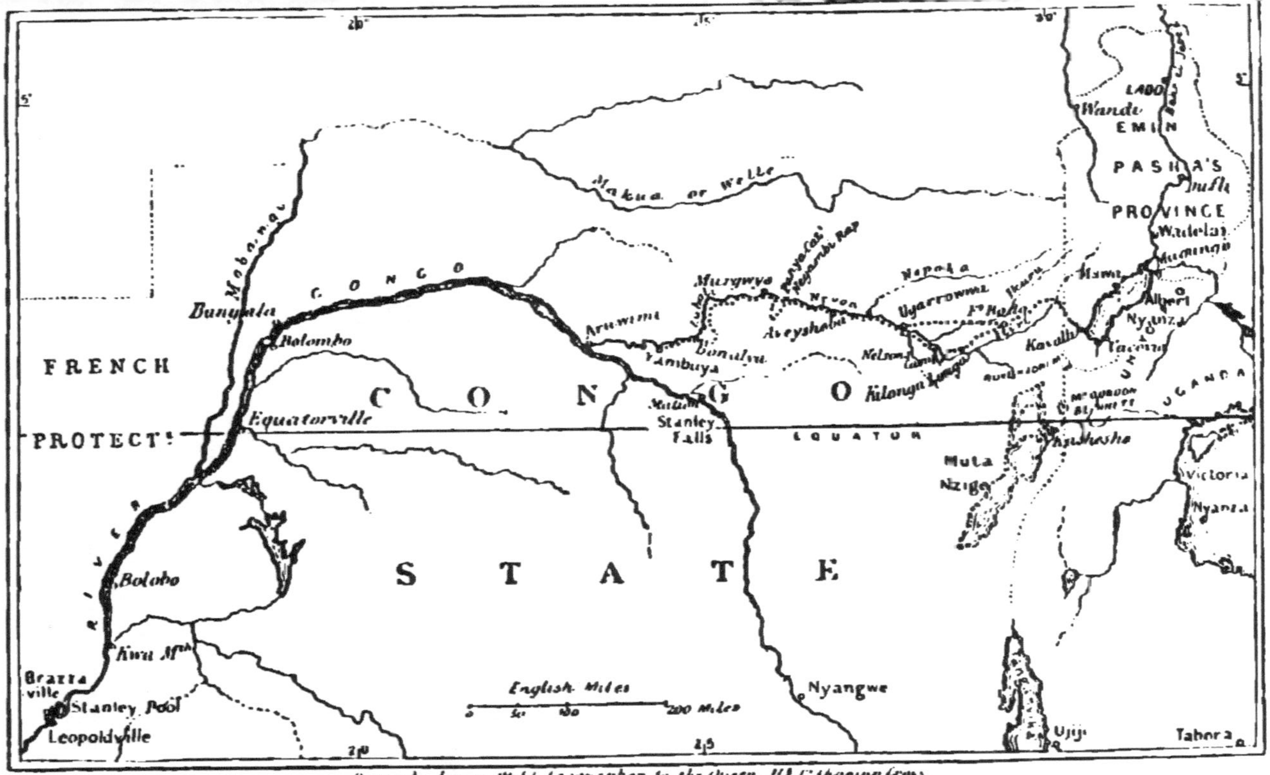

Drawn by James Wyld Geographer to the Queen, 11 & 12 Charing Cross.

THE RELIEF OF EMIN PASHA.

MAP OF THE ROUTE TAKEN BY H. M. STANLEY.

EMIN PASHA.

CHAPTER I.

INTRODUCTORY.

A PRESENT-DAY philosopher of repute says of heroism, that it is the self-devotion of genius manifesting itself in action. If this is so, and if valour is the part of men, then Eduard Schnitzer—EMIN PASHA—deserves to rank with the truest heroes of the present or any century. His name, in fact, already belongs to the history of these times.

The unique spectacle of a solitary European holding his own, for years, against hordes of fanatical and implacable foes, and boldly carrying on a desperate struggle, single-handed, for liberty and humanity in the very stronghold of African barbarism, has aroused the sympathy and called forth the admiration of the whole civilised world. Soldier and scientist, diplomatist and pasha, engineer and surgeon, the chief executive officer of a vast and populous Egyptian state, and the valued correspondent of the principal learned societies of Europe, the biographer of this illustrious servant of science and humanity on the Dark Continent will be at a loss under what category to put him.

Those who have lived with Emin, and shared his labours on the banks of the White Nile, declare that he seems to be born to that only which he goes about, so dexterous is he in all his undertakings in camp, in hospital, in the desert zareba, in council, with sword, with pen.

The secret of Emin's heroic self-denial and masterly devotion to duty is his unswerving loyalty to, and reverence for, *a memory*—the memory of the Hero of Khartoum, erewhile his friend and fellow-worker in the splendid enterprise of freeing Central Africa from the blighting curse of the slave-hunters.

As the last surviving lieutenant of the great Englishman in the Egyptian Soudan, Emin believes that it now rests with himself alone to preserve the name of GORDON, and the glorious traditions which surround it, fresh and fragrant and potent in the heart of Equatorial Africa, and to carry out, as best he may, the policy which that name and those traditions represent.

"Upon me," he wrote in 1887, "as his—Gordon's—last surviving officer, devolves the great honour of carrying on his work and developing his intentions, and be sure that, by God's will, I shall succeed."

Untrained in the science of arms, a member of a peaceful and learned profession, gentle and refined by nature, with a lofty idea of duty, and an unselfish charity and patience, which have deeply impressed all who have fallen beneath the spell of his personal influence, the Pasha has laboured "with both hands" to promote the best interests of the dusky millions of Inner Africa. So far he has kept secure the key to the greatest slave-hunting region on the entire continent.

Like Gordon, Emin believes that it is his life-duty to employ himself in the emancipation of the black races of the equatorial regions, and with a fine courage and cheerful heart, and unquenchable hope, he has gallantly held his province, since the fall of his leader—his *ideal man*—amidst the ruins of Khartoum, steadily refusing to leave his post, thinking only of the multitudes of helpless natives who look to him as their only hope, and, as he says of himself, "throwing care to the winds, and looking for better times."

Notwithstanding the wail which we hear at times for the chivalry that is no more, it may fairly be asked whether the career of this simple German surgeon is surpassed by anything recorded in the annals of the nations.

With his example before us, we need not yet despair of our race. On the contrary, it should inspire us with the conviction that the best and purest glow of chivalry is not dead, but that it vigorously lives among us yet, and that there are still left to us strenuous souls, who cherish

> "The king-becoming graces:
> Devotion, patience, courage, fortitude."

CHAPTER II.

EARLY DAYS.

EDUARD SCHNITZER, known to fame as Emin Pasha, was born at the quaint little Silesian town of Oppeln, in Eastern Prussia, on March 28, 1840. His father, Ludwig, was a wool-stapler, in a fair way of business. Both Ludwig Schnitzer and Pauline his wife were Protestants and Lutherans. In 1842, the family removed to Neisse, where the relatives of the heroic Pasha still reside. At an early age young Eduard, a delicate and sensitive lad, was sent to the gymnasium, or public school of the town, where he remained for some years. In 1858, he left Neisse to enter upon a course of medical study at the University of Breslau. Like most German students, Schnitzer did not remain stationary at one university, but attended lectures at Berlin, Vienna, and Paris. To go to the tavern to drink lager beer, to sing songs, and to fight duels, is a part of the curriculum of a German student; but it must not be supposed that Schnitzer did naught at this period of his life but carouse and swell those rough choruses of festive song with which every visitor to the university towns of the Continent is familiar. An ardent naturalist, and a lover of science, the young Silesian was already laying the foundation for that accurate knowledge of languages and the phenomena of physical life, which has since earned for him the respect of the chief *savants* of the day. After a course of technical instruction in surgery and physiology in the hospitals of the German capital, he graduated, taking out his diploma as doctor of medicine in 1863-4. Schnitzer had always evinced a decided taste for travel and a love for the study of natural history, and as soon as he was free to follow his own inclinations, he decided to follow "the spirit of movement" which was upon him, and set out to seek some sphere of congenial work in a foreign land. He determined to see the world before settling down, and turning southward, he made his way to Constantinople, where his skill and intelligence and modesty of demeanour attracted the notice of the Turkish officials, and soon gained him many friends in the capital of the Sultan. But Constantinople did not hold Schnitzer long. He wandered into Syria, and upon the recommendation of his friends at the Sublime Porte, was eventually appointed to the post of surgeon of the staff by Ismail Hakki Pasha, the Governor of Scutaria and the adjacent provinces. On the death of Hakki in 1873, Schnitzer resigned his appointment and returned to Europe. Retracing his steps homeward, he spent several months of 1875 at Neisse, where he employed himself in severe linguistical study, and natural history and scientific research. Plants, animals, and the various specimens of organic life that he had collected in his travels, were dissected and examined with patient ardour by the young biologist, and his labours in this direction, at this period of his career, did not pass unnoticed by the learned societies of Germany. Wearied, however, by the dulness and monotony of life in an obscure provincial town, the ex-staff surgeon of Hakki Pasha made his way to Egypt. Reaching Cairo in 1876, he offered his services to the Khedive Ismail, who sent him up the Nile to Khartoum with orders to report himself to the Governor-General of the Soudan. Schnitzer, who had now dropped his Frankish name, and adopted the Egyptian cognomen of Emin—the Faithful One—was invested with the subordinate rank of Effendi in the native army on his arrival at the Soudanese Capital, and appointed to act as surgeon-general to Gordon Pasha, then Governor of the Equatorial Provinces of Egypt, the garden of the Soudan, a vast area of fruitful country of almost illimitable extent and of inexhaustive wealth, with a teeming population, magnificent water-ways, and a climate by no means disagreeable to Europeans. The province had been added to the dominions of the Khedivate in 1870-73 by Sir Samuel Baker, who established the seat of government at Gondokoro, and annexed the entire country as far south as the Equatorial Lakes to the Egyptian Soudan.

CHAPTER III.

GORDON AND EMIN.

WHEN Mohammed Ali, in 1820, determined to subdue all the countries lying south of Wady Halfa and add the Soudan to Egypt, his avowed object was to introduce civilisation and trade into the heart of the African continent, and, by these means, to pacify the Negro and Arab tribes of the great fertile belt of country which lies between the Sahara and the Lake Region. It was soon found, however, that slaves paid better than ivory or gold or grain, and slave-hunting was carried on in the Nile Valley by the Egyptians to such an extent that the indignation of Europe was at length aroused by the horrors of these slave raids. The Government at Cairo connived at the atrocities committed by the gangs of armed man-hunters, who destroyed villages and depopulated whole districts, to supply the slave markets of North-East Africa, and made a substantial profit out of what was, in fact, a royalty. The basin of the White Nile, as far south as the Victoria Nyanza—the queen of African lakes—was the happy hunting-ground of the slavers, and the field of their most profitable operations. The Khedive Ismail, under pressure from England, made an attempt to suppress the abominable traffic, but he was defied by the notorious Zebehr, the arch man-stealer of the Soudan, who defeated an expedition sent up by the Khedive to crush him and put an end to his nefarious practices. With a view to checking the ravages of this Lion of the Desert, who had established an independent court and set up the insignia of royalty in his capital, at Darfur, General Gordon was selected to succeed Sir Samuel Baker as Governor-General to the newly-annexed Equatorial Provinces in 1874.

Before leaving Cairo for the White Nile, the General, with his usual perspicacity, had read the real motive of Ismail in sending him up to Gondokoro, the capital of the new province. Gordon roundly declared his belief that the zeal of the Khedive for the suppression of the slavers of the inner Soudan was "a sham to catch the attention of the English people." But the resolute Englishman, fresh from his brilliant campaign at the head of the "ever-victorious army" in China, was determined to proceed upon his mission of mercy to the myriad populations of the equatorial regions, and after some "skirmishes" with his superior officer, the Governor-General of the Soudan, at Khartoum, with reference to the adoption of a "forward" policy against the slave-hunters, Gordon sailed up the Nile for his capital, after publicly declaring his fixed determination to establish throughout his provinces a government monopoly of the ivory trade, to prohibit all imports of arms and powder and the levying of armed bands by private persons, and to set up a rigid passport system, which would virtually put the whole territory from the Bahr-el-Arab to the equator under martial law. Gordon could trust none of his subordinates. He suspected, and as it proved rightly, that they were all more or less committed to the slave-trade, and that every official about him shared covertly in the spoils of the man-hunting expeditions. He felt the responsibility and peril of the task he had taken in hand, viz., to crush and root out this abominable and growing evil, but "I will do it," he said, "for I value my life as naught, and should only leave much weariness for perfect peace." Gordon managed, in spite of the anxiety which pressed upon him and the sense of loneliness that at times overpowered him, to get some fun out of his voyage south to take up his new dignity. One night a peal of laughter from a thicket by the water-side startled him. "I felt put out," he said, "but the irony came only from birds that laughed at me from the trees in a very rude way. They were a species of stork and seemed in capital spirits, and highly amused at anybody thinking of going up to Gondokoro with the hope of doing anything." On his arrival he found the Egyptian occupation of the region limited to the possession of a few military posts. The capital of his province was in a state of siege. The country was "up" on all sides. After the departure of Sir Samuel Baker any government beyond the range of the guns of the forts had ceased to exist. The peaceful native villages had been raided and robbed by the Egyptian officials, cattle had been driven off, and the owners reduced to slavery, and shipped down the river to the markets at Khartoum, Berber, and Assuan, and Gordon found, to his infinite disgust, that the worst offender was the redoubtable Raouf Pasha, the very commander from whom he was to take over the reins of government. Dismissing his predecessor without honour, the General set to work to bring order out of chaos. He strictly enforced his own decree as to armed bands and ivory trading, and the importation of arms and powder and the production of passports, and he had some of the chief law-breakers sent off in chains to Khartoum, where they were either set at liberty or secretly assisted to escape by the Governor-General of the Soudan.

Gordon, who had been given full powers within the area of his own satrapy, now planned and carried out two successful campaigns: one against the slave-traders south of Kordofan, who were instigated to rebellion by Zebehr, the other in Darfur. The romantic incidents of the operations which followed, and the remarkable personal influence which Gordon exercised, are matters of history. He succeeded in breaking up the slave-traders' organisation and in giving the traffic in human beings a serious blow, and in securing, for the time, the vast riverain population of the Nile Valley and the Negroes of the southern districts from the ravages of the nomad Arab tribes, who swept like a flood into the equatorial Soudan, from the region between the Nile and the Red Sea.

The English Pasha's difficulty was with his own subordinates, a body of Circassian, Turkish, and Albanian adventurers, who had to be provided for by the government of Cairo, and who were appointed to the offices of collectors of revenue and heads of districts in the remotest provinces, with a view to satisfying their claims upon the Khedive without any further trouble and outlay on the part of the Egyptian authorities, at the expense of the long-suffering and patient black people in the far Soudan. These men intrigued against their white chief and "checkmated" him at every turn. His life was in constant danger, and he lived, as he himself described it, "within a ring-fence of scoundrelism." He found that his chief local officer at Gondokoro had connived, on one occasion, at the passage of a convoy of one thousand six hundred slaves down the river for the "consideration" of three hundred and sixty dollars. The Khedive was writing to him "quite harshly" to put an end at once to the transport of slaves from his province to the Red Sea routes. The Khedive's officials were helping it on. But the courage and ability and integrity of the most remarkable man that Africa has ever seen, told in time upon the mass of corruption and brutal callousness to human suffering, by which he was environed, and before the end of the second year of his administration he had established and garrisoned eight new stations; he had carried peace and security for life and property to the extreme borders of his principality; he had effectually pared the claws of the Lion of the Desert; and he had dealt a crushing blow at the prestige of the most wealthy and powerful slave-dealers by the vigorous enforcement of martial law everywhere within the limits of his government. His rule was impartial and just. The natives first trusted and then reverenced the white Pasha, who had burst their bonds from their necks and bearded the dreaded Zebehr in his den in the desert fastnesses of Darfur. The Egyptian officials did not love the upright, fervent man, but they at least soon learned to fear him, and the heart of Ismail was made glad by the receipt in due course at Cairo, for the first time in the history of the province, of a substantial tribute from Gordon's state, which was paid into the national exchequer, and which had been collected from the contented and prosperous people in the far away Nile Valley without injustice and without violence. Villages were built up again in the open country, fields were tilled, herds of cattle roamed over the fertile plains of the vast territory in perfect security; old roads, long deserted and "killed," were once more traversed by bands of merchants and solitary passengers, conveying their goods and the produce of their gardens and pastures from market to market; the native industries revived and flourished, and there was every promise of the dawn of a long day of peace and prosperity and contentment for Gordon's "children" in that beautiful Nile basin, which Sir Samuel Baker describes as "the future granary of the world," and as a region which, in a few years, under good government, would supply corn and cotton alone sufficient to make Europe independent of any other quarter of the globe. The General, though only a soldier, was at once impressed with the luxuriance of the vegetation and the boundless wealth of "the pearl of the Soudan." "An almost virgin soil, a tropical sun, the Nile water, and *a population which is most tractable and peaceable* :"—"Here," he said, "were all the elements required to make the equatorial Soudan the richest and most productive region in the entire African Continent."

To save this magnificent country from being scrambled for by the filibusters and pirates of the world, and to prevent its becoming from end to end a vast field for piratical adventure, tribe fighting against tribe, and slave-hunts decimating the population, and throwing back the fairest districts into sterility, and the whole region into chaos—this was the arduous work that the second White Pasha of the Equatorial Provinces set himself to carry out, and this was the splendid task which he eventually accomplished.

The arrival of Emin Effendi at Gondokoro was a matter of intense satisfaction to General Gordon. That masterful but tender man, who combined sweetness with strength, in the administration of his rapidly-growing and improving state, at once found in the quiet, unobtrusive and somewhat reticent German doctor, a man after his own heart.

CHAPTER IV.

EMIN AS A DIPLOMATIST.

THE English soldier and the German surgeon became inseparable companions. The high sense of duty and simplicity of character displayed by the newcomer struck both natives and foreigners alike, and we gather from his journals, written at Khartoum, that Gordon held his *fidus Achates* in high esteem, not only for his scientific accomplishments, but for his innate sagacity and quiet resolution, and for his marvellous "grip" of all the great African questions.

Dr. Emin was employed by the General in a variety of ways, not strictly professional, and on several occasions he was sent upon tours of inspection to the heart of the province, to report upon the condition of the people, reform abuses, review the garrisons, and exercise judicial functions as the representative of the great Pasha himself. Soon after being joined by the doctor,

Gordon decided to establish a line of stations right down to the shores of the Victoria Nyanza, to enter into a treaty of amity with the powerful M'tesa, the Emperor of Uganda, and to proceed south to arrange some matters that were in dispute with Kabrega, the sovereign of the Unyoro country. A formidable expedition set out, therefore, in 1876 from Lado, a town on the left bank of the Nile, to which Gordon had transferred the seat of his government on account of the insalubrity of Gondokoro. A visit of ceremony was paid to the court of M'tesa, who was described by Mr. H. M. Stanley, in his story of the discovery of the Congo, as the "Hope of Central Africa." The region of the Great Lakes had to be explored in detail, and garrisons established to protect the people from the raids of the slavers. Early in the spring of 1876, therefore, the little column was threading its way *viâ* Fatiko, through "a dreary country strewn with outcrops of iron ore, and with slag from the native smelting." The region was a lonely, swampy desert of marsh and slime, out of which, "the moment the sun goes down, a cold damp arises that enters one's very bones." But the resolute, well-drilled "blacks" tramped bravely on over the weary miles of malarious bog. The thorns tore the clothing of the two Europeans to rags, and gigantic elephants cumbered the sinuous and gloomy paths through the almost impenetrable thickets. The wary monarch of Unyoro was already on the alert, and with the first tidings of the approach of the White Pasha he fled from his capital, carrying off, at the same time, the "magic stool," and burning his palace and treasure-houses. Gordon was equal to the occasion. He at once placed Riongo, a nominee of his own, upon the vacant throne, and having left garrisons of his "faithfuls" to support the new monarch in his future struggle with the recreant Kabrega, the expedition went on its way, and after surveying Lake Albert and the adjacent country, returned in triumph down the Nile to Khartoum, where Gordon and Emin were for some time engaged in taking active measures against some slave-dealers who had their headquarters in that city. In 1877, Dr. Emin was sent down to Unyoro to accept the homage of the penitent Kabrega, who had succeeded in rcovering the supreme power, and who was anxious to make his peace with the White Pasha of the North. Proceeding without escort to Unyoro, Dr. Emin carried out his mission with such success that quite recently, Kabrega, of his own free will, sent up a supply of stores to the doctor, and the friendship between the two men has proved invaluable to Emin, who has been often able to send letters through the Unyoro country, when all the rest of the continent has been closed against him. It was also out of respect for Emin that Kabrega assisted the famous Russian traveller, Dr. Junker, to escape from Uganda three years ago, and to leave inner central Africa *via* Unyoro for Zanzibar.

The mission to Uganda was one of singular difficulty and peril. M'tesa, the then reigning monarch, was a savage at heart, and capable of the most fiendish acts of cruelty when enraged or thwarted in his schemes. An Egyptian officer, acting contrary to Gordon Pasha's instructions, had marched with three hundred men to the capital of Uganda, with the intention of annexing the dominions of M'tesa! The Pasha's men were at once secured by the well-disciplined battalions of the sable emperor, and the chances were that M'tesa would order them, in a paroxysm of rage, to be massacred in cold blood. Emin was sent to appease the furious king and bring back the men, whose lives had been placed in such fearful peril by the folly of their leader. The task was accomplished with complete success, and without firing a shot.

Emin paid a second visit to Uganda, and such was the impression made upon the fiery and formidable M'tesa by the silent, thoughtful German, that it is said of Emin in Uganda to this day, that he was the only white man for whom the Emperor had ever shown any sign of respect or fear. The negotiations entrusted to Emin were often of a delicate and intricate nature, and the physical force at his command was never sufficient to hold its own for an hour in the face of serious opposition, but Gordon's emissary had caught the spirit of his master. He knew how to deal with the "black man," and on one occasion a diplomatic arrangement with one of these semi-barbarous kinglets, on the borders of the Equatorial Provinces, undoubtedly saved Gordon Pasha and his soldiers from certain annihilation.

The General and the doctor twice visited the Lakes in company, and they also carried out, on one occasion, an important survey of the country east of Foweria, "a dead, mournful land, with a heavy damp dew penetrating everywhere; as if the angel Azrael had spread his wings over the place. No words can picture its silence and solitude. The river was navigable up to the foot of the Murchison Falls, and then began an arduous tramp in the pouring rain, through dense jungle, and terrific ravines coming down laterally from the table-land into the deep canyon in which the river ran." Five days' scrambling through a tangle of wild vines and other creepers at the rate of eighteen miles a day brought the party, under the command of the General himself, back to Foweria, and the survey was complete. The road was then followed south as far as Speke's Nyamyango, eighty miles farther in the direction of the Victoria Nyanza, and a tract of virgin country, equal in area to Ireland, was annexed to the Equatorial Provinces in the name of the Khedive.

In December, 1876, Gordon left Lado and proceeded to Cairo, and resigned his post as Governor of the Southern Soudan. The results of his labours, however, remained. He had managed, in less than two years, to reorganize and develop the state, to crush out the slave-raiders, to purge the administrative department, and to restore peace and confidence among the various races under his rule where before all had been anarchy and confusion. He had swept away a heavy debt that he found resting upon the province and had re-opened the markets right across Africa, from the Niger to the Nile, so that ivory, grain, rice, and cattle were once more freely offered everywhere for purchase by the native chiefs. He had established a postal system, opened up friendly relations with neighbouring and independent states, and had left behind him an imperishable name, not only as a military commander of dauntless courage and great strategic skill, but as a philanthropic civil administrator of no mean practical ability.

CHAPTER V.

GOVERNOR OF THE EQUATORIAL PROVINCES.

IN 1878, General Gordon was back at Khartoum, with the title of Governor-General of the Soudan, and with the supreme control over Darfur, the Eastern and Western Soudan, and the Provinces of the Equator, vested in himself by royal firman. He had applied, at Cairo, for leave to select three sub-governors to assist him in the administration of the vast state committed to his charge. His request was granted, and he was, at the same time, desired by the Khedive Ismail to give his chief attention to the suppression of slave-wars, and to do all in his power to open up direct and well-protected trade routes to the most distant confines of his extensive satrapy.

Dr. Emin Effendi had remained on the White Nile, after the departure of Gordon in 1876, as surgeon-general to the Khedival forces, and he was immediately chosen by the Governor-

General to fill the important post of supreme executive officer in the Provinces of the Equator. With the rank of Bey, the new administrator at once took up the reins of government. During the interval between the resignation of his former chief and the appointment of Emin Bey, the affairs of the territory had been under the control of a number of Egyptian officers, with the usual results. The state was once more deeply in debt. The slave-traders had reappeared, and slave-raiding was going forward everywhere unchecked. Villages were depopulated, the markets were deserted, trade roads were "killed," and the various tribes inhabiting the most fertile region in the world were again at strife with each other. Plunder, rapine, and excessive taxation had exasperated the natives, who were in a condition of sullen discontent and incipient rebellion, and the outlook was altogether one that would have tried the faith and damped the courage of any ordinary man. But Emin girded and braced himself for the struggle. He made a rapid tour of his new dominion. He dismissed every official convicted of oppression or dishonesty. He disbanded the Egyptian troops, and enlisted the "blacks" of the province to serve under him. He fell upon the slave-raiders, wherever he could find them, with the suddenness of a thunderbolt and the force of an avalanche, and dealt out stern punishment to all who were convicted of any breach of the "Gordon Code," which had become the law of the land years before, and had never been annulled by Khedival decree.

With astonishing energy this single-hearted man swept over the broad territory between the Sahara and the Lakes, at the head of his black battalions, and in time reduced order out of chaos once more, by a marvellous display of "one-man" power. When not actually on a journey, he spent his days, from sunrise till sunset, in hearing appeals and complaints, and in the administration of justice. He granted audiences to the meanest of his subjects. All communication with Khartoum was stopped for years by a block on the river, and his people were frequently in a lamentable condition for want of seed-corn and food supplies, till their own crops had matured. But the indefatigable Bey went everywhere, inquiring into everything, and attending to the needs of all, allaying discontent, equalising taxation, clearing the prisons, rebuilding the stations, and securing obedience to the authority of the Khedive.

In 1882, he reported his province as pacified. The deficit of £32,000 which he found when he became Governor had disappeared, and there was a balance of £1,200 to the credit of the state. The cultivation of indigo, cotton, rice, wheat, and coffee had been encouraged and developed, confidence had been restored, and the "Garden of the Soudan" was once more blooming and fruitful.

Day by day Emin went quietly but steadily on, doing what his hand found to do, patiently and well. His first visit, on leaving his quarters at daybreak, was always to the hospital at Lado, where he listened to the reports of the various cases and examined the patients, as carefully as if no cares of state of any kind pressed upon him. Nothing could induce him to leave or neglect his hospital work. But in the pursuit of his favourite recreation, his natural history experiments, he constantly allowed himself to be interrupted, saying, with a quiet smile, "Business always before pleasure." Schnitzer is a born naturalist. His studies of African flora and fauna have long interested the scientific world, and the valuable results of his zoological and botanical researches have received, from time to time, the warm commendation of such experts as Dr. Gustav Hallant, of Bremen, Dr. Felkin, of Edinburgh, Professor F. Ratzel, and Dr. Junker.

In 1878, a well-known traveller met the now famous Pasha—he was then Emin Bey—in a block on the Nile. "I well remember," he says, "going aboard his (Emin's) steamer, and the warm reception he gave us. Dressed in a white uniform and wearing a fez, he presented the appearance of a tall, thin man of military bearing. The lower part of his face was hidden by a well-trimmed, black beard, and a moustache of the same colour partially veiled a determined mouth. His eyes, though to some extent hidden by his spectacles, were black, piercing, and intelligent; his smile was pleasing and gracious; his actions graceful and dignified, and his whole bearing that of a man keenly alive to everything passing around him. Courteous, but reserved, he was distinguished as a thorough gentleman. He addressed us in English, but subsequently finding I spoke German, we conversed in that language. Emin is a remarkable linguist, having a knowledge of most European languages, and of several of those spoken in Asia, and of many African dialects."

The scientific reports which have reached Europe from time to time from the accomplished Governor of the Southern Soudan have been always remarkable for their minuteness and accuracy of detail. They are expressed in elegant language, and written in a hand of exquisite neatness, and so faithful is the description of places and trees and flowers, and all the manifold phenomena of African tropical life, that, to use the expression of one of the most gifted of the Pasha's correspondents, "one can even hear the buzz and feel the sting of the insects" he writes about.

CHAPTER VI.

LIFE AT LADO.

EMIN BEY truly lived laborious days. At sunrise, on his way to prescribe or operate at the hospital, he reviewed his troops on parade, and at night, when the cares of government were over for the time, and his weary lieutenants sought well-earned repose, you would see him writing, by the light of candles made by himself, those delightful papers on scientific subjects that enrich the pages of so many learned periodicals. Anthropology, botany, geology, and philological questions, all came alike to him, and served to occupy the odd moments of his scanty leisure ; and in addition he contrived to find time to teach his people the arts of weaving, training oxen for the yoke, waggon-making, road-building, and the cultivation of wheat and indigo, and various other useful and profitable cereals and plants. Lado, his capital, was in happier times a well-built, well-ordered town, with its divan, offices, mosques, and government buildings, all constructed with burnt bricks and roofed with corrugated iron, the other houses in the town being of wood and glass. The place stands on the bank of the river opposite to Gondokoro (Ismaili), the city "founded" in 1860 by Sir Samuel and Lady Baker. The streets are wide and straight, and surrounding the station there was a broad promenade, a clear space of a hundred feet kept between the houses of the people and the earthworks and fortifications. Beyond these were large gardens. The capital had three gates, at which sentries were mounted day and night; the gates being open from 6 A.M. till 8 P.M. No gun was allowed to be fired near the walls from sunset to sunrise, unless as a signal of attack. At 5.30 A.M. the bugle sounded the *réveille*, and shortly after, "Light your fires." At 6 A.M. the muster-roll was called, and the gates were opened. The soldiers were then drilled, and the women began to sweep the streets; for Emin took strict precautions with regard to sanitary matters, a point at which the African village system, as a rule, breaks down, and the people were taught in a practical way that "cleanliness is next to godliness." At 8.30 A.M. all, excepting the sentries, turned out to work in the fields, to draw water, to fetch wood, and, the dew by this time being dried up, the cattle were sent out to graze. Work lasted till 11.30 A.M., when there was an interval of rest till 2.30 P.M.; the people then set to work again till 5 P.M., when all returned inside the walls. At 8.30 P.M., the roll was called, and the gates shut, and at 9 P.M. all fires were extinguished, an officer going the rounds to see that the regulations were carried out. Curfew in Central Africa is a very important precaution, for, should a hut once catch fire, the whole station is doomed to destruction. In the spring of 1878, before Emin's rule began, Lado was burnt to ashes, and all the valuable reserve stores, which Sir Samuel Baker had taken up to the province, were destroyed.

Emin has never for a moment departed, in his attitude towards the natives, from the Gordon tradition. He has a high opinion of the capacity of the "blacks," or native races of the Soudan, over whom he rules, and the chiefs trust him to a man. On taking service in Africa, as we have seen, he sank his Frankish origin, as far as possible, in order to carry out the policy of Gordon and identify himself with the people. In a letter to his sister, in 1876, Emin says: "Here I have already gained a reputation as a doctor. This is due to the fact that I know Turkish and Arabic as few Europeans know them, and I have so completely adopted the habits and customs of the people that no one believes that an honest German is disguised behind the Turkish cognomen of 'Emin.'" But the Bey was no renegade or half-hearted Christian, nor one of those Europeans who rave about the advantages of Mohammedanism over Christianity as a civilizing agent in Central Africa. He is in thorough sympathy with Christian effort, and speaks in his letters home with something like scorn of Islamism, which had not, he said, to his certain knowledge, made one convert in twenty years in the whole area of his province. One of the most striking characteristics of the man has been his display of strategic and military skill. The news of the fall of Khartoum, conveyed to him by his braggart foes, with an invitation to lay down his arms and embrace the creed of the Mahdi, was a painful blow to the hopes of the Bey. The death of his friend and chief, beneath the blackened ruins of his own capital, only seemed, however, to act as an incentive to Emin to hold his territory, at all hazards, for the sake of his people, against the savage hordes of the false prophet. "The death of Gordon," he wrote on August 16, 1887, "has been a great blow to civilization in Africa. Certainly he would have done better to have made his way here, where friends awaited him. Through prisoners we have heard of his arrival in the Soudan, but we never could make out what he was doing, and the news of the fall of Khartoum, and of Gordon's death on the 21st of January, given me by the Mahdi's commander, Keremallah, seems too incredible for acceptance.* Gordon has his rest; he died, as he wished, the death of a soldier *Now it is our duty* to carry on his work."

* It will be remembered that Ismail abdicated in 1879, and was succeeded by his son Tewfik Pasha. The new Khedive and Gordon did not see "eye to eye" in matters of administration, and the latter, therefore, resigned the Governor-Generalship of the Soudan and returned to England. He afterwards served in China, India, and the Cape, and in 1884 he was deputed by the British Government to return once more to Khartoum to arrange for the evacuation of the entire Soudan by the Egyptians.

CHAPTER VII.

DARK DAYS.

WITH the surrender of the Soudanese capital and the death of its intrepid defender, in the early days of 1885, the triumph of the Mahdist legions in North-East Africa seemed to be complete. The wave of civilization that had begun to flow down towards the equator was ruthlessly driven back, and the power of Egypt was completely destroyed and overthrown below the region of the Second Cataract. The return of the Nile Expedition and the fruitless campaign of General Graham at Suakim closed a chapter in the history of the "Land of the Blacks," which opened only seventy years ago with the conquest of the Soudan country by the fierce but valiant sons of Mohammed Ali, the founder of the reigning Khedival dynasty. The unfortunate garrisons planted here and there in the desert were abandoned to their fate. Some of them, as Kassala and Senaar, held out bravely against the savage levies of the Mahdi till starvation and want of ammunition made resistance no longer possible. Some of the "faithfuls," with their families, reached Dongola after the fall of Khartoum, but several of Gordon's white lieutenants, *e.g.* Slatin Bey, the erewhile Governor of the Bahr-el-Ghazel, Lupton Bey, Mr. Frank Power, some Greek officials, a party of Austrian missionaries, and nuns and others, were taken prisoners by the Mahdi's generals, and reduced to a condition of degradation, and in some cases even of slavery. Lupton died in chains, of privation and misery, and the condition of the other Europeans in captivity was, and is still, one of unredeemed wretchedness and hopelessness. With the relapse of the Northern Soudan into anarchy, and the abolition of any form of settled government, people seemed to imagine that the entire region had been abandoned and given over to the spoiler. Such, however, was not the case. Though much had been lost, all was not lost. The Pearl of the great Soudan country—the Equatorial State—was still intact. Thrown upon his own resources, Emin Bey, on hearing of the rise of Mohammed Ahmed, and of his pretensions to a divine call to drive out the Egyptians and al white men from the country, at once set to work to strengthen his position, to arm and drill his troops, and fortify a position at Wadelai, south of Lado, on the left bank of the Nile, and to provision his stronghold in anticipation of any attack that might be made, sooner or later, upon him. In his distant station he heard from time to time of the startling events that were transpiring away to the north. Truculent messages reached him occasionally from the Mahdi, assuring the vigilant Bey that his turn would soon come, and that there was no chance of his escape, with his handful of Egyptian and Negro troops, unless he accepted the authority of the Mahdi, and donned the coat of a Mohammedan dervish or devotee to the faith of Islam. To these communications the reply of Emin was one of proud defiance. Trusting in God and the righteousness of his cause, the resolute German kept careful watch, night and day, across the desert for the first signs of the rise of the banners of the prophet upon the horizon northward. All communication between Wadelai and the outer world was completely broken off. North and south and east and west the tiny fortress, with its solitary banner floating to the winds, was hemmed in by wide stretches of desert waste, and there was no possibility, even if the desert could be crossed in safety, for any messenger to penetrate the cordon established by the Mahdi, or to pass his vidcttes with any letter or tidings of the beleaguered Bey. A cloud of darkness and mystery gradually settled over the Equatorial Province and its faithful administrator. Rumours reached Europe, as the months passed away, that Emin was still holding out, but that the tide of war was rolling southward down towards the equator, and that one of the generals of the second Mahdi was ascending the Nile with a powerful flotilla in order to attack Wadelai and crush for ever the power of the dauntless Emin. Still no definite news of the fate of the Bey and his loyal little garrison broke the complete and painful silence which now enveloped the region. The worst was often feared. But for four years, unaided by supplies, and unsupported by a single word of sympathy from the outside world, Emin stood his ground, and never lowered his flag, although hardly pressed at times and almost driven to despair by the sufferings of "his children" from famine and his own want of the ordinary necessaries of life. Surrounded by bitter foes, the single-hearted White Chief infused enthusiasm into the hearts of his followers day after day, and at length the news reached England, by letter from Wadelai from Emin himself, that up to July, 1886, he had bidden defiance to the Mahdi, and held his own against the slave-raiders and the disaffected negro tribes that troubled his borders. The letter had taken four months and a half to reach England from Wadelai, and it had been got through the heart of Africa to Zanzibar by Kabrega, the King of Unyoro, already mentioned in these pages.

Emin's story was a thrilling recital, and worthy of a friend of Khartoum Gordon. Trouble there had been, and sorrow upon sorrow. Sickness and want and disease had thinned the ranks of his noble troops; gaunt and haggard, and without shoes or uniforms, they had kept watch and ward upon the ramparts of his little fortress; and they had at length been face to face with "the insolent foe." So far, however, they had stood unmoved and undismayed. Their ammunition was woefully lessened, however, and the question was whether they could hold out till relief reached the banks of the White Nile from Europe, or Cairo, or Zanzibar. An outburst of sympathy followed the publication of this letter from the besieged Bey. It was determined that some attempt should be made to relieve him, and to supply his most urgent needs. At the meeting of the British Association at Manchester, in 1887, Sir Francis De Winton, the able successor of Mr. Henry M. Stanley in the administration of the Congo Free State, said:—"Public attention has recently been much concerned in the fate of Emin Pasha. [Emin had been raised to the full rank of Pasha by the Khedive Tewfik immediately on hearing of the gallant defence which his representative was still waging for his Government in the south.] Sent to the southernmost limit of the Egyptian conquests on the Nile by the late General Gordon, Emin Pasha, a German by birth, had governed the province committed to his charge with signal success and ability. After the fall of Khartoum, he was cut off from all communication with his Government, and for four years he has, unaided, withstood invasion from without and disruption from within. But he is now in want of supplies and assistance, and last year an urgent appeal from this brave man reached England through the Church Missionary Society. This appeal, as you know, was not passed by unheeded. If you look at the map, you will see that the territory governed by Emin lies between the two great slave-dealing centres of Equatorial Africa—that of the Bahr-el-Ghazel, extending into the Niam-Niam and Monbotto country, and that of the region of which Tanganika, Nyangwe, and Stanley Falls are the centres. Thus the possession of the territory occupied by Emin becomes a very important factor, as in this wise it not only checks the advance southwards of the Bahr-el-Ghazel traders, but it effectively prevents the junction of these two slave-dealing centres, whose operations were surely and steadily approaching each other. Think for a moment what would have been the result of such a junction! A trade would have been immediately opened to the north, thousands of slaves would have been employed carrying the ivory tusks, and every species of cruelty would have resulted. Khartoum would in time have become a large market, and the unfortunate creatures who survived the horrors of the journey from the south would be again obliged to carry the ivory to the coast, or perhaps across the Syrian desert. Now mark what this means; it means that the Mahdi and his followers are supplied with a valuable commodity with which they can trade, and obtain in exchange the European goods they so much need; it means they can obtain a plentiful supply of native recruits; in short, it means that *a great central Mohammedan power would have been established in Central Africa.* And this is what Emin has striven to prevent, for now neither the Arab trader of the Bahr-el-Ghazel, who is in communication with the Mahdists in the north, or those of the Upper Congo, can obtain powder and other ammunitions by which alone they can carry on their cruel and nefarious traffic. Without fire-arms they cannot hold their own against the natives, now that the net is slowly but steadily gathering round them. The Germans on the east, the British on the north-west, the Congo Free State on the west, and Emin Pasha, like a wedge, thrust into their midst—it will be the fault of civilised Europe if this country and its population are to be handed back again to the slave-raiders. How faithfully and how successfully and with what ability Emin Pasha has fulfilled the trust committed to him is well known, and has excited the admiration of Europe. In him are to be found the spirit and the gentleness, the charity and *the devotion to duty* which so strongly characterised his late commander, and it was the possession of these qualities which, no doubt, drew them towards each other, and which led General Gordon to advance him to his present command as Governor of the Egyptian Equatorial Province. It seems to me that the work he has performed in the past, and the work he has set himself to accomplish in the future, must play an important part in the history of Central Africa."

CHAPTER VIII.

THE EMIN PASHA RELIEF EXPEDITION.

FROM October, 1886, to the early days of 1888, nothing more was heard of Emin. The cloud, which had lifted for a moment in the autumn of the former year, and showed us the heroic Pasha, pressed sorely by his enemies, and in dire need of succour, yet undismayed, in his river stockade in the inner heart of Africa, once more fell over the fateful Nile valley, and for a year the distressing silence was unbroken. The plan for a Relief Expedition, by way of Zanzibar or the Congo, was pushed forward. Funds were freely offered. A Government subsidy was guaranteed by the Council at Cairo, and the Royal Geographical Society generously made a grant of £1000 towards the fitting-out of the Expedition.

The command of the Expedition was placed in the hands of the man most capable of conducting it to a successful issue—Mr. Henry

Morton Stanley—and in January, 1887, the main body of the Relief Party left England for the Congo, the route chosen by the commander of the enterprise for his advance upon the far-away desert station of Wadelai. A few days before he left London for Africa, Mr. Stanley was presented with the freedom of the City, and in speaking of his plans at the banquet at the Mansion House, in reference to the toast of his health, he said, "I am leading an expedition into the centre of the Great Continent for the relief of an Egyptian officer, who is in straitened circumstances and environed by breadths of unknown territory, populated by savage tribes. The borders of these unexplored lands are occupied by people actively opposed to this officer's retreat or to any communication with him. Others are hostile through sheer barbaric ignorance, and passively opposed to the advent of strangers. We are not going to annex anything. We shall not excite the peoples of Africa, or endanger the safety of the missionaries, or arouse the susceptibility of the Germans. If we go by the Congo route, the King of the Belgians has nobly placed the whole naval stock of the Congo Free State at my disposal for the purposes of the Expedition for ninety days. I intend to proceed at once to Zanzibar, recruit a force of followers, and leave for the Congo immediately, if I find a steamer ready to take us to Banana Point. If not, I shall strike inland for the Albert Nyanza, and I shall not rest till I have got news of Emin, unless I perish in the attempt." These resolute and weighty words plainly showed that Mr. Stanley had a pretty clear idea of the country through which he intended to travel, and of the kind of people he would have to deal with on the road to the Equatorial Province. By the Congo route the whole party were conveyed by water to within 800 miles of Wadelai. The route from the east coast inland would have necessitated a painful and tedious march of 1,200 miles, partly through the openly hostile kingdom of Uganda, in order to reach the shores of the Albert Lake. The undertaking bristled with difficulties at every step; the broad belt of country between the Congo and the Nile had never yet been traversed by the white man. It was a veritable *terra incognita* to the explorer. The course of the Expedition, after leaving the Congo, would lie through the great zone of forest land which occupies the heart of the continent. It was known that the people of this region were the most fierce and relentless cannibals in Africa, and possibly in the world, and that the endless and gigantic forest growth which stretches from the head-waters of the Zambesi to the Soudan might delay the party for months and even years. The task of leading a caravan into the heart of Africa is, under the most favourable circumstances, a hazardous one, and every precaution that experience, and sound judgment, and prudence could suggest, was taken by Mr. Stanley for the comfort and safety and success of the party. The daring heroism of the leader of the Relief Expedition was universally acknowledged. It was felt that the man who in former days had found Livingstone would in due course find Emin Pasha, and the movements of Mr. Stanley and his party were eagerly followed with the deepest interest by the people of both hemispheres. Mr. Stanley spent the day before leaving England at Sandringham, the country house of the Prince of Wales, where the famous traveller explained to his royal host and hostess and their children his plans for the conduct of the important mission entrusted to him by the Emin Pasha Relief Fund.

Having recruited a large party of baggage porters, and men for his armed escort, at Zanzibar, he arrived at the mouth of the Congo in June, 1887, with a force, all told, of considerably over 900 men. An English traveller, who met the Expedition on its way up the Congo, says

"I was on my way down country to embark for England. About two days from here (Bangala), I met two armed Assyrians, or Soudanese. Immediately behind them, and mounted on a fine mule, whose new plated trappings glistened in the sun, was Stanley himself. Behind him strode a Soudanese giant, about 6 feet 6 inches high, bearing a large American flag. I saluted the 'Congo King.' He smiled, and, indicating the bare ground, said, 'Take a seat.' We squatted accordingly. He handed me a cigar. We talked for about half an hour. He was very nice and kind. He accepted me as a volunteer (I had previously written to him), and it was at once arranged that I should proceed down to this place, and see to the transport of some of his remaining loads. I have done so, and now have to overtake him in four days. Of the eight whites he has with him, two [Mr. Jamieson, of Dublin, and Mr. Jephson] have contributed to the expenses of the Expedition, for the privilege of accompanying Stanley through 'the heart of Africa.' Others are English army officers who have come out as volunteers. I never in my life was so much struck with any sight as with Stanley's caravan on the march—Egyptians, Soudanese, Somalis, Zanzibaris, and others, 900 strong. It took me two hours to pass them, and then I met the second in command, Major Barttelot, a young fellow, burnt very dark, with a masher collar fixed on a flannel shirt, top-boots, &c. He was carrying a large bucket that some fellow had abandoned. 'I say, are you ——?' he shouted. 'I am ——,' I said, 'and I now belong to the Expedition.' 'I am very glad to hear it,' he replied; 'Stanley has written to you, and so you are coming along; that's right! Very good business!' He seemed very fit, was full of tremendous spirits, and I admired him immensely. Tippoo Tib, the notorious slave-trader of Stanley Falls, has come round from Zanzibar with Stanley, and in his silken robes, jewelled turban, and kriss, looks a very ideal Oriental potentate. It is thought 'good business,' as Major Barttelot would say, getting him for an ally."

A strongly fortified and entrenched camp was established at Yambuya, on the Lower Aruwimi, a tributary of the Congo, flowing almost east and west, at the highest navigable point, just below the First Rapids. Major Barttelot, the senior officer under Mr. Stanley, was appointed commandant; Mr. J. S. Jamieson, a Dublin gentleman of considerable scientific attainments, was associated with him. Messrs. Bonny, Ward, and Troup were also attached to the staff of the Major, and he was left with a force of 257 men at the base of operations, and a full supply of reserve stores and ammunition, which was to be sent on later, for the use of the main column.

The Major was to remain at Yambuya until the arrival of the steamer from Stanley Port, with the officers, men, and stores still on their way up the Congo, and on the arrival of Tippoo's promised contingent of carriers from the Falls Station, the Major was to set out with the stores, and march his column on the track of the main body till he came up with Stanley. The blazed trees and forsaken camps and zarebas left by the main column were to guide him as to the line of march, and if Tippoo's men did not arrive by a fixed date, he was to leave part of the heavy baggage behind, and press forward by double and triple marches to join Stanley on the road to Wadelai.

CHAPTER IX.

STANLEY TO THE RESCUE.

ON June 28, 1887, the advance column, consisting of 389 officers and men, set out from the Aruwimi to push its way on towards the Albert Nyanza. At first the natives opposed the march of the white man's caravan, but their resistance did not cause any loss of life or seriously hinder the progress of the party. After following the sinuous course of the Aruwimi for some time, an inland path was taken, which trended east. For five days the column kept to this road, which led through a country densely populated by hostile tribes, who fired their villages as the expedition approached, and exhausted every art known to the native mind for molesting, impeding, and worrying an enemy. The march was, however, continued without the loss of a man. From the 5th of July, when the river bank was once more followed, till the 18th of October, the friendly waters of the Congo tributary were never out of sight. On the 1st of August, serious trouble, in the shape of dysentery and fatal sickness, seized the gallant little army, men began to fall out and desert by the way, and when for nine days the road lay across a sterile, savage wilderness, man after man fell out by the roadside, and perished of sheer weariness or famine. The river, as in the years before, when tracing the then unknown windings of the Congo Lualabu, again proved a friend to Stanley. He placed his sick and disabled followers in canoes, and was thus enabled to make steady, if not brilliant, progress. On August the 13th, the pioneers of the force announced that the natives in front of the tiny host were bent on opposing their further progress. In the struggle which ensued Lieutenant Stairs was hit with a poisoned arrow in the region of the heart, and Mr. Jephson, in leading a relief party to the assistance of his chief at a critical moment in the fray, lost his way and led his men inland. All were happily reunited again on the 21st, and on the 25th of August the column arrived at the junction of the Nepoko with the Aruwimi. For the first time Stanley now came face to face with the Arab slavers, led by Ugarrowwa, *alias* Uledi Balyaz, who turned out to be a former tent-boy of Speke's. "Our misfortunes began," says Mr. Stanley, "from this date, for *I had taken the Congo route to avoid the Arabs*, that they might not tamper with my men, and tempt them to desert by their presents. Twenty-six men deserted within three days of this unfortunate meeting." On the 16th of September the expedition suffered terribly, owing to the scarcity of food in the vast district round the Arab station of Ugarrowwa, which had been depopulated and devastated by this man and his well-armed followers. Sixty-six men had been lost by death or desertion, and fifty-six men, including all the Somalis, were left at this place, invalided, or indisposed any longer to face the hardships of the march to the yet distant Nyanza. On the 18th of October the station of Kilonga-longa, a Zanzibari slave of Abed-bin-Salmi—an Arab whose bloody deeds are referred to in "The Founding of the Congo Free State"—was reached, and here fifty-five more men left the column. The servants of this Arab also tampered with the rapidly diminishing host of Stanley, purchasing their rifles, ammunition, and clothing, so that when the party left the station they were beggared, and some of the men were absolutely naked. Still "onward" was the order of the day, and with a brave heart, bursting with suppressed indignation, the gallant leader of this perilous and arduous enterprise faced bravely on for the White Nile. The men were now so weak physically that they were unable to carry the boat they had contrived to convey so far on their journey, and the useful little craft, with seventy bales of goods, was left, under the charge of Surgeon Parke and Captain Nelson, at Kilonga-longa's village. For some weeks the diet of the men had been fungi, wild fruit, and a large, flat, bean-shaped ground nut. The slaves of Abed-bin-Salmi, who did their best to ruin the Expedition, short of open hostilities, had carried devastation and death everywhere, in a vast region which extended to within a few miles of Ibwiri—not one native hut standing between Ugarrowwa's and Ibwiri: the whole region was one horrible wilderness. Beyond Ibwiri, however, the party was out of reach of the destroyers; it was on virgin soil, in a populous region, abounding with rice, and pleasant fruits, grain, and food of every kind. The famine period, which began on the 31st of August, ended on the 12th of November. Out of 389 men only 174 were left, and a halt was ordered for the men to recuperate. Hitherto the poor people had been sceptical of what was told them about the purpose and end of the mission. Their sufferings had been so awful, their calamities so numerous, the forest so apparently endless, that they positively refused to believe that they would by-and-by see the teeming plains and uplands, and flocks and herds, and banana fields by the Nyanza region, and behold the great White Pasha, Emin, about whom all the world was talking. The men turned a deaf ear to the entreaties of their commander and his officers. Driven by hunger and suffering, they sold their valuable rifles and equipments for a few ears of Indian corn, deserted with the cartridges, and were altogether demoralised. Seeing that prayers and mild punishments were no longer of any avail the extreme penalty of death was resorted to, and two of the worst cases were accordingly taken and hung in the presence of all. Thirteen days were spent in Ibwiri, where the miserable band of attenuated wanderers revelled on fowls, goats, bananas, corn, sweet potatoes, yams, beans, &c. The supplies were inexhaustible, and the people glutted themselves. Hope returned, and brighter views of life; and Stanley with pride remembers that the effect of this abundance of food upon the 173 men left to him was marvellous. "I set out," he says, "for the Albert Nyanza on November the 24th with a body of followers who were positively sleek and robust men." On the 5th of December the Expedition emerged upon the plains, and the deadly, gloomy forest was at length behind it. After 160 days of continuous gloom, they saw once more the full, clear light of the broad day shining down upon them and making all things beautiful. "We had never seen," says the great traveller, "grass so green or country so lovely. The men literally leaped and yelled for joy as they raced over the ground with their burdens." They were like new creatures as the fresh, cool breezes of the open plain swept over them and about them. Woe betide the enemy now that should attempt to stay the progress of the party! With such a spirit in them, the men would fling themselves like wolves on sheep. Numbers would not be considered. It had been the eternal forest that had made the abject, slavish creatures so brutally plundered by Arab slavers at Kilonga-longa's town. On December 9th, the force arrived in the country of the mighty chief Mazamboni, "a lord of many villages," where the rich plains and river's bank were studded with large clusters of well-built huts, surrounded by fields of corn and carefully cultivated patches of banana and sweet potato. From a long distance the natives had sighted the caravan, and were prepared to give it a by no means friendly reception. Stanley at once seized upon a hill and threw up a strong zareba, behind which he placed his men, and awaited the turn of events with considerable anxiety. Was it to be peace or war? If peace, then well; but if war, how would it end? The inequality of the combatants, should Mazamboni put his legions into the field and decide to fight the strangers, was simply ludicrous. Stanley took in the position, as the hero of many an African fight, and the zareba, built of brushwood and deeply entrenched, was hastily strengthened, as the war cry of the enemy arose with terrible volume upon the wind, and was sent pealing from hill to hill and across the intervening valleys on all sides of the beleaguered force. The people gathered by hundreds from every point in response to the summons of their chief. Hours passed away. Both parties were on the alert, but the peace had so far not actually been broken. Mazamboni professed to be subject to Kabrega of Unyoro, the friend of Emin, and Stanley hoped that if the purpose of their mission was made clear to these people they might be allowed to go on their way in peace. A present of brass rods and cloth was made up and sent off to the doughty chief, all hostile demonstrations were suspended, and the night of the 10th was spent in awaiting the reply of Mazamboni as to whether it was to be "kanwana" or "kurwana"—peace or war—between himself and the white strangers. Early on the morning of the 11th, the shout of the natives, in the valley below the zareba, rose up indistinctly to Stanley as he waited to catch the word which rose and fell upon the breeze. Which was it, "kanwana" or "kurwana"?—the sounds, so terribly different in meaning, were so provokingly alike in articulation. Presently a native came up to the zareba with the news that it was "kurwana"—war! and, that there might be no mistake, two arrows were shot into the little extemporised fort. There was no time to lose. With splendid tactical skill, Stanley at once set about to make the most of his little army. Jephson, with a smart, picked body of thirty rifles, was sent to the east to test the courage of the attack in that quarter. Stairs, who had recovered from his wound, went with forty men to attack the valley, where the enemy were already mustering in hundreds. The plan of the affair was altogether aggressive. The expedition, instead of awaiting attack on its own ground, sallied forth and fell upon the astonished enemy, and before nightfall the way to the Nyanza was open. On the morning of the 12th the march was continued, and during the day the party were engaged in four fights for the right of way. On the 13th the path was due east; and in the face of hourly attacks from all quarters the advance was pushed forward, till, at fifteen minutes past one on that eventful day, after many weary months of wandering and suffering, and bloodshed and weariness, by flood and forest and field, Stanley turned proudly and excitedly to his little host, and cried, "Prepare yourselves for a sight of the Nyanza!"

CHAPTER X.

STANLEY AND EMIN MEET.

THE men murmured and doubted, as they trudged on, beneath the blaze of the tropical sun, with unwilling feet and drooping spirits. "Why does the master continually talk to us in this way? Nyanza, indeed! Is not this a plain, and can we not see mountains at least four days' march ahead of us?" At 1.30 p.m. the Albert Nyanza was below them, spread out, as far as the eye could trace it, like a shield of burnished gold. Now it was the turn of the leader of the little company to laugh at the doubters, and ask them what they saw. The poor fellows were wild with astonishment and joy. They threw themselves, in true Oriental fashion, at Stanley's feet, and strove to kiss his hands, as they humbly begged him to pardon them for their waywardness and incredulity. The gallant pioneer now had his reward. The expedition had reached an altitude of 5,000 feet above the sea. The Albert Nyanza was over 2,900 feet below the delighted travellers, who stood in 1 deg. 20 min. N. lat.; the south end of the lake lying largely mapped out about six miles south of this position. After a short halt to enjoy the prospect, the rugged, stony descent to the shore was commenced. But the long-looked-for end was not to be gained without a sharp struggle. The natives poured down upon the party from all quarters, but the courage of the strangers was equal to the occasion, and, with a desperate effort, the Nyanza plain was reached, and a camp formed at the foot of the plateau wall. The expedition next morning approached the village of Kakengo, at the south-west corner of the lake. The people were not actively hostile, but refused to have anything to do with them. Emin had not been able to get down to the point at which Stanley expected to meet him, and as the latter was without boats or any means of traversing the Lake northward to Wadelai, the only feasible plan seemed to Stanley to be to return to Ibwiri, build a fort, leave a garrison in the fort to hold it, and raise corn for the marching column; return to the Albert Nyanza, and send the boat in search of Emin, who had possibly had no news whatever of the movements of the force sent for his relief. This plan was determined upon after a long council of war, and the next day the return was begun, Ibwiri being reached on January 7th, 1888.

Meanwhile affairs in the Equatorial Province had taken a turn for the better. During the time occupied by the Relief Expedition in reaching Central Africa from the mouth of the Congo, Emin had not only managed to re-establish his authority in his territory, but he had been able to take the field successfully against his foes on several occasions. He had received a peremptory summons from Khartoum to disband his forces and to surrender himself to the officers sent against him by the Mahdist leaders. The messengers bringing the summons had also presented a letter to the Pasha, purporting to have been written by Lupton Bey, then a prisoner at Khartoum, declaring that he supported the proposal of the rebels, and saying that Emin's surrender was the only means of saving the lives of the Europeans then in chains at Khartoum. It was also announced that a strong force was marching on Wadelai, and that the massacre and extermination of Emin's troops was inevitable. Emin at once declared Lupton's letter to be a forgery, and when the Pasha had positive information of the approach of the enemy, he was preparing to advance to the attack, without waiting for the hostile force to reach Lado. The energy of Emin's tactics disconcerted the Mahdists, and in the end he was left to reorganize his territory without further serious molestation. The receipt of the following letters from Wadelai considerably allayed the anxiety in the public mind as to the position of the Pasha during the past two years :—

"WADELAI, *August* 16*th*, 1887.

"DEAR MR. ALLEN,—

"Your most welcome letter of 19th November, 1886, reached here at the end of June, 1887, and I should have answered it at once had I not been detained by a month's work on the western shores of Lake Albert. A new station which I pushed towards the south needed inspection, and a little caravan with goods from Uganda had to be brought home. Forgive, therefore, the delay, and accept my thanks for your considerate and cordial words.

"Convey, also, please, my and my people's heartiest thanks to the Anti-Slavery Society. Their ready sympathies with our position, their unselfish advocacy of help to be sent, their generous exertion in our behalf, have greatly rejoiced and obliged us, and our warmest thanks will never equal our obligations. As to myself, if ever I wanted an encouragement to pursue my work, the acknowledgment of what, by God's permission, I was allowed to do until now will spur me to go on and to do my duty cheerfully.

"I am sorry to disappoint your kind wish that your letter may find me safely arrived at Zanzibar, and I may as well tell you that I have been greatly amused by the doubts expressed in some papers if I would stay or leave when Mr. Stanley arrives. I think there can be no doubt that I stay, and I wonder how one could suppose the contrary. I need not dwell on the reasons for my decision; would you desert your own work just at the dawn of better times?

"Since my last letter to you I have been able to resume the regular turn of affairs, relaxed somewhat by the events you know. I have inspected our stations, and erected two new ones. I have put order everywhere, and our native chiefs have been consulted. The crops of this year are luckily abundant, the cotton plantations yield very fairly, and altogether things look now more brightly than before. By Mr. Mackay's kind help I have procured a considerable lot of sheeting and prints from Uganda; if not sufficient to cover our wishes, they were enough for giving to everybody some little gift. But as our self-made 'damoor,' or cotton stuff, is more appropriate for wear and tear, we reserve these for holy-days. The value of what they receive I make my men pay from their wages.

"I cannot speak too highly of the untiring exertions and valuable assistance afforded me by Mr. Mackay, the Church Missionary in Uganda. At great personal inconvenience he has not only provided for the despatch of our posts from and to Zanzibar, and done his utmost to facilitate our transactions in Uganda, but he has actually deprived himself of many valuable things to assist myself and give me comfort. He has done splendid work in Uganda, but lately his labours have been somewhat interfered with by the Arabs trying to have him turned out of Uganda. His position, therefore, has become dangerous, but I hope he may be able to hold his own. In the interest of the Uganda Mission, I am very glad that Mr. Stanley chose the Congo road for his expedition. He will there encounter numberless difficulties, arising mostly out of the soil to go across; yet he will without doubt succeed in vanquishing them; whilst, coming by Uganda, he would never have obtained permission to come here, except by sheer force, besides imperilling the life and work of the missionaries."

The letter then proceeds to express the mind of the Pasha as to the future, in the following touching words:—

"Once provided with the necessaries, I deem it not at all difficult to open a direct road to the sea coast by way of the Lango and Masai countries. A chain of stations in suitable places and distances is more than sufficient for holding the road open, and the country itself is so rich in camels and donkeys, and so eminently fit for breeding them, that means of transport will never want. The only obstacle to conquer is the fierceness of the Lango people. I think, nevertheless, that by cautious and energetic proceedings they may become more manageable. I should like, respecting this, to hear the opinion of Mr. Thomson, whose book I have not yet been able to procure.

"At all events, you see, I have a good lot of work before me, and if, with God's help, I succeed in carrying out only a part of it, I shall feel more than rewarded for whatever I have had to undergo. Privations do not terrify me—twelve years' stay in Central Africa are a good steel.

"The death of Gordon has been, as you truly say, a great blow to civilisation in Africa. Certainly he would have done better to make his way here, where friends awaited him. Through prisoners, we had heard of his arrival in the Soudan, but we never could make out what he was doing, and the news of the fall of Khartoum, and of Gordon's death there, on the 21st of January, given me by the Mahdi's commander, Keremallah, seemed too incredible for acceptance. Gordon has his rest: he died, as he wished, the death of a soldier—now it is our duty to carry on his work, and upon myself, his last surviving officer in the Soudan, devolves the honour to develop his intentions. Be sure that, by God's will, I shall succeed.

"The King of Uganda is again at war with Kabrega, who would not listen to my warnings, misled as he was by an Arab trader.

"The whole western part of Unyoro has been laid waste. Kabrega had to escape, and is now somewhere near Kisuga, on the road to Mrooli. The Waganda established themselves in Mayangesi, and seem unwilling to quit the district again. All communications are closed. I do, therefore, not know when I may be able to forward this letter, but I trust it will reach you safely some day or another. Do not forget your promise to write to me sometimes,

"And believe me to be,

"Yours very faithfully,

"DR. EMIN PASHA.

"*To the Secretary of the*

BRITISH AND FOREIGN ANTI-SLAVERY SOCIETY."

"WADELAI, *October* 25*th*, 1887.

"DEAR FRIEND, ... In my last letter I told you how Mahomet Biri arrived with the second caravan of goods. . . . I have been prevented sending him back to Uganda owing to the amount of war which still exists between Uganda and Unyoro. . . . The Arabs will only make use of the situation in obtaining a higher price for the gunpowder they manage to smuggle into Unyoro. Will the introduction of gunpowder from Zanzibar never be stopped? The one who really suffers most from these everlasting quarrels is myself. The route to Uganda is rendered almost impracticable. Sometimes, it is true, Myanga permits the Arabs to send people to me; at other times he forbids them to do so. Kabrega addresses all the people who come as spies, has their goods examined, and confiscates all correspondence which he sees. It is due to this fact that since May 2, 1887, I have never had a single letter from Mr. Mackay, and I do not even know whether he is still in Uganda or not. . . . On the 22nd of September I was able to send letters to Mr. Mackay, and I am in hopes he has received them. In a few days it is my intention to go myself as far as Kibiro, taking Mahomet Biri with me to that station. Kabrega is sending some of his officials to confer with me. There is little enough to be gained by these conferences. To be sure, when all is said and done, Kabrega does as he likes or as his advisers for the time being suggest. I expect that I shall gain permission to Biri to pass through Unyoro. If I had only sufficient soldiers at my disposal they would enable me to obtain very speedy concessions to my requests and wishes. If Mr. Stanley arrives, as I hope he may do, in November, many of my difficulties will be done away with, not that I intend to undertake another warlike enterprise. That is very far from my desire, but the mere fact that I have received them will, I confidently expect, soon bring to an end all the quarrels among my childish neighbours. . . . If I cannot report that our relations with Unyoro and Uganda are satisfactory, I can say that the chiefs nearer me are more friendly. Chief Befo, of Mount Belinian, near Gondokoro, who played such a great *rôle* in the last Bari and Ormka revolt, has just sent me some broken rifles as a present, and has also requested a conference. He is undoubtedly the most important of the Bari chiefs, and he is also the most cunning, and I greatly wish it was in my power to accede to his request. I should do so, were it possible for me to visit him, but in the meantime I feel it my duty to remain here. . . . My sphere of action has been greatly confined to Lake Albert, but I have made some days' journey to the west towards Alandu, and I intend, as soon as I come back from Kibiro, to pay a short visit to some of the friendly chiefs in that district.

"All goes well personally. I have to thank Mr. Mackay for many little luxuries. By last caravan he sent me some of Wills's best bird's-eye, and you can imagine what an unexpected present this was for one like myself, who for years have been cut off from such articles. With regard to my personal state, I may tell you you need not have any anxiety about me. As soon as I have become aware of the possibility of now and again corresponding with you and with one or two others, I have tried to throw care to the winds, and look with a certain amount of confidence to better times in the future."

In a postscript, dated the Island of Aunguru, October 31, 1887, Dr. Emin Pasha writes:—

"At last I arrived here the day before yesterday. To-morrow I take Mahomet Biri by steamer to Kibiro. From there he goes to Bjuaia, where he will remain with Captain Casati until Kabrega sends him the necessary powers. This will probably occupy three weeks, although I will use every endeavour to expedite matters. Biri has promised that directly on his arrival at Casati's he will send one of his people on with my post to Uganda, so that it is just possible they may return with letters before he leaves Casati's. I calculate with some certainty upon his doing this, because up to the present he has proved himself pretty reliable. If he is delayed in Unyoro I shall probably return from my Alandu visit before he leaves. I have . . . sent on this occasion several boxes full of collections of birds, &c., to the British Museum, addressed to Professor Flower, and I hope he will find not a few interesting specimens among them. I have not been able to send a quantity of very valuable objects, as the cases and boxes have come to an end. I have been compelled, therefore, to write to the Professor asking him to send me supplies, which I hope he will do, and not object to these requests, which I only make on account of my isolation."

In a second postscript, dated November 2, 1887, from Kibiro, Dr. Emin Pasha writes :—

"Everything has now been arranged, so that Mahomet Biri started to-day. We have had very bad weather. Storms and rain have prevailed, so that the steamer had very hard work. Kibiro lies exposed on all sides to the winds; therefore I cross over the lake to-morrow to M'soa, where I shall establish my camp and send the steamer back to Wadelai. In a few days my journey commences to Walendu. Biri's people take this letter. Excuse its length. Write as often as you can find time, for the only holidays I get are those days on which letters come from you.

"(Signed) DR. EMIN PASHA."

After a few days' rest at Ibwiri, Stairs was sent off with a hundred men to bring up the boat from Kilonga-longa's, with the stores left there, under the charge of Surgeon Parkes and Captain Nelson. Out of the thirty-eight sick left at the village in October, eleven only accompanied their officer to Ibwiri with the boat; the rest had died or deserted. On April 2nd, the journey back to the Nyanza commenced. The natives, including Mozamboni, were now friendly, and every difficulty seemed to vanish. Food was supplied gratis; cattle, goats, sheep, fowls, and rice were given in such abundance that the people lived royally. A day's march from the Lake, a messenger arrived with "a black packet" for the white man, which he said had been given to him by another white man, "Malezza," to give to "his son," the leader of the strangers. "If your words are true," said Stanley, "I will make you rich." Wonderful stories were told by the messenger of "big ships, as large as islands, filled with men," &c., which left no doubt in the mind of the commander of the relief column that this white man, "Malezza," was Emin Pasha. The note was handed up, covered with a strip of black American oilcloth. It was from Emin, and was to the effect "that as there had been a native rumour to the effect that a white man had been seen at the south end of the Lake, he had gone in his steamer to make inquiries, but had been unable to obtain reliable information, as the natives were terribly afraid of Kabrega, king of Unyoro, and connected every stranger with him. However, the wife of the Nyamsassie chief had told a native ally of his, named Mogo, that she had seen Stanley in Inminsuma (Mozamboni's) country. He therefore begged Stanley to remain where he was till he (Emin) could communicate directly with him." The note was signed "(Dr.) Emin," and was dated March 26th, 1888. Mr. Jephson was at once sent off in the skiff, towards the north, and met the Pasha at the Egyptian Port of Mswa, his southernmost post on the Nyanza. The boat's crew were embraced one by one, and were hailed as brothers by the assembled garrison. On the afternoon of April 29th, at 5 P.M., Stanley, who had re-occupied his old camp at the south end of the Lake, saw the *Khedive* steamer, about seven miles away, steadily making for the bivouac. Soon after seven o'clock, Emin Pasha, with Signor Casati and Mr. Jephson, landed on the beach and met with a magnificent welcome from the Relief Expedition. Stanley had much to tell and much to hear. The two men, thus strangely brought face to face in the heart of the great African continent, had each a marvellous and pathetic story to relate, and they remained together, discussing their plans for the future, till the 25th of May. The work of the Emin Pasha Relief Expedition was completed, for, in spite of the most earnest solicitations of the courageous leader of the enterprise, the faithful Pasha resolutely declined to quit the province. The Egyptians with him were, he said, anxious to get back to civilization, but the blacks were ready to remain with him. He feared the relapse, once more, of his province into anarchy and barbarism if he left his post, and he had made up his mind, as we have seen in his letters already given, to cast in his lot with his people.

The Pasha had two battalions of regulars under him—the first, consisting of about 750 rifles, occupied Duffle Honya Laboré, Muggi, Kirri, Bedden, Redraf; the second battalion, consisting of 640 men, held the stations of Wadelai, Fatiko, Mahagi, and Mswa, a line of communications along the Nyanza and Nile, about 180 geographical miles in length. In the interior, west of the Nile, he retained three or four small stations—fourteen in all. Besides these two battalions he had quite a respectable force of irregulars, sailors, artisans, clerks, servants. "Altogether," he said, "if I consent to go away from here, we shall have about *eight thousand* people with us."

"Were I in your place," said Stanley to the Pasha, "I would not hesitate one moment, or be a second in doubt what to do."

"What you say is quite true, but we have such a large number of women and children—

probably ten thousand people altogether. How can they all be brought out of here? We shall want a number of carriers."

"Carriers! carriers!—for what?"

"For the women and children. You surely would not leave them, and they cannot travel."

"The women must walk. It will do them more good than harm. As for the little children, load them on the donkeys. I hear you have about two hundred of them. Your people will not travel very far for the first month, but little by little they will get accustomed to it. Our Zanzibar women crossed Africa on my second expedition. Why cannot your black women do the same? Have no fear for them; they will do better than the men."

"They would require a vast amount of provision for the road."

"True; but you have thousands of cattle, I believe. These will furnish beef. The countries through which we pass must furnish grain and vegetable food."

"Well, well; we will defer further talk till to-morrow."

CHAPTER XI.

MAJOR BARTTELOT. FAITHFUL UNTO DEATH.

IT will be remembered that early in 1888 unfavourable news of the Relief Expedition reached the camp at Yambuya, through several deserters from the force, one of whom had returned in bad health to a village situated a few miles from the station. Some Arabs returning from the mountainous region of the Upper Aruwimi had also reported to the camp at Yambuya having met deserters from the pioneer column, among them being two Soudanese, who formed part of the personal escort of Mr. Stanley. According to these men, disaster had overtaken the force, and its leader had been severely wounded by an arrow, and was lying helpless and deserted in a village far away in the interior. Reports of a more circumstantial nature even soon followed, to the effect that Stanley was dead, and the relief party scattered and massacred to a man. A fresh and powerful expedition was at once organised by Major Barttelot to go forward on the track of the pioneer caravan, and test the truth of these startling rumours, and the Major left the camp at Yambuya on May 10 with the object of rejoining Mr. Stanley. The caravan accompanying Major Barttelot comprised 640 carriers, recruited by Tippoo Tib, and 100 soldiers, the latter forming almost the whole military force left by Mr. Stanley at Yambuya, before his departure for the interior, to guard the camp. Two other officers, with Mr. Jamieson, accompanied Major Barttelot and shared between them the command of the column, the advance guard being under Mr. Jamieson's charge. It was Major Barttelot's intention to follow Stanley's march step by step. At the date of the departure of the caravan for the interior, no news had yet reached Yambuya direct from Mr. Stanley. Major Barttelot's carriers were very heavily laden with supplies, brought partly from Leopoldville, and partly furnished direct by Tippoo Tib, and it was believed that the advance would consequently be very slow. The same messenger who brought the above news announced that Captain Vangele, accompanied by two other white officers and a detachment of 50 soldiers, retook possession of the Stanley Falls Station on June 4, on behalf of the Congo Free State. They met Tippoo Tib there, and found his authority and that of the Congo Free State were respected. At the time of the return to Aruwimi of the steamer which conveyed Captain Vangele to Stanley Falls at the end of June, the detachment of 40 men left by Major Barttelot to guard the camp at Yambuya had heard no news of Stanley. They had only received advices from Major Barttelot to the effect that the first stages of his march had been satisfactorily accomplished.

In a report to Mr. Mackinnon, dated August 15, 1887, Major Barttelot said: "Since Mr. Stanley's departure, Mr. Jamieson and myself have been employed in fully carrying out his instructions. The trench has been dug, the platforms put up, the bank of the river cleared, and the clearing to the east side kept clear. I have ascertained the position of all villages within a four-mile radius on the southern, eastern, and western sides. Our relations with the natives are most friendly. They trade with the men in a small way, and the chiefs come in constantly to see us. Lately they have come to claim our protection against some marauding Arabs, who may or may not be Tippoo Tib's people. I have tried to ascertain, but cannot obtain any information. The steamer *Stanley* arrived yesterday,

August 14, with Messrs. Troup, Ward, and Berry, three donkeys, and 479 loads. Our present strength is—Soudanese, 44; Somalis, 2; Zanzibaris, 200; total 246. The sentry duty is entirely furnished by the Soudanese, the Zanzibaris only finding pickets. Up to the time of writing this, Tippoo Tib's men have not arrived, though these marauding Arabs before mentioned may be them. Should it turn out to be so, or should they eventually come, I shall march at once in Mr. Stanley's track. If, however, they do not, I shall be compelled to stay here till November, when Mr. Stanley expects to return, or till such time afterwards as he may return. Since Mr. Stanley's departure our casualties have been: Soudanese, 1; Somalis, 2; Zanzibaris, 4; total, 7. Attached is a sketch of the camp by Mr. Jamieson, which will show you everything for the safety of the camp as regards the fortifications. Attached also is a copy of the camp orders for your information, which will show you that all has been done to preserve discipline, alertness, and cleanliness."

The Major had been directed to keep open the lines of communication between Stanley and the Congo and Europe, to send on supplies at once, in case of need, to the main force, and to be ready to receive Stanley again should he return by that route. Unfortunately, however, there was one part of his duties which he was never in a position to perform—the sending on of letters from Stanley to England—for the simple reason that no communication reached him from the day almost that Stanley left the river to plunge into the unexplored region, where his further movements were soon shrouded in mystery and silence. Breaking up his camp, therefore, the Major resolved to do all that could be done to succour his leader, if he was yet alive, and he took to the river route to find Stanley. This news afforded a certain amount of relief to the anxious friends of the great explorer, but the hopes raised by the energetic action of the Major were shattered by the intelligence, some weeks after, that Barttelot had been murdered by his carriers, and had fallen a victim to his own zeal and devotion, and added another name to the already long list of notable men who have given up their lives, almost with joy, as a sacrifice on the altár of humanity.

On July 28, at noon, while the officers at Stanley Falls were lunching, Tippoo Tib arrived in a very excited and agitated state. He had just heard of the assassination of Major Barttelot by his Manyuema carriers, some hours' journey beyond Nurenia on the Aruwimi.

In August, Mr. Jamieson arrived in a small boat at the Falls, having gone to confer with Tippoo Tib, and to make known the details of the disaster. The following is the account given of how Major Barttelot came by his death:—

The Manyuema natives have a habit of beating drums and singing late in the evening and early in the morning, and there was no means of preventing them from continuing this practice. Major Barttelot, who had made several days' journey with his caravan of four hundred men into the interior, objected very strongly to this noise, and even used threats in the hope of stopping it. Nevertheless, on July 19, at four in the morning, the drumming began, whereupon Major Barttelot became very angry, and went out of the hut, which he occupied in common with Mr. Bonny. In spite of the advice of the latter, Major Barttelot said he would stop the drumming, and went to the hut of the man who was beating the drum. He had scarcely reached it when suddenly a shot was heard. Mr. Bonny ran out, and saw all the people in camp rushing about, and crying, "M'Zonngou Kufna!" ("The white man is dead"). Mr. Bonny made a search in all directions, and found the body of Major Barttelot lying in front of the drummer's hut, the breast pierced by a bullet. The clothes showed marks of burning with gunpowder. The following day Mr. Jamieson, who was with the advanced guard, was informed of what had happened, and he arrived back in the camp and restored a little order. All the men forming the caravan had, however, dispersed, and all the loads of beads and stuffs had been stolen.

Mr. Jamieson, who afterwards died of fever at Bangalas, returned to the Aruwimi camp with the *débris* of the caravan, and then came on to Stanley Falls to make arrangements with Tippoo Tib. He left Mr. Bonny with such of the men as had been caught and all the provisions which had been saved at the Aruwimi camp.

The official report goes on to say that there is no doubt of Tippoo Tib's good faith. Major Barttelot on several occasions when he came to Stanley Falls Station, was warned by the officers there, as well as by Tippoo Tib, to treat the men of the caravan with leniency and not to resort to flogging. In continuation, the report says that the deceased officer was a man of great spirit, endowed with indomitable courage and energy. His health was excellent. By means of forced marches he had accomplished the first stages of his advance into the interior with extraordinary rapidity.

Mr. Jamieson declared to the officers at the

Falls Station that Major Barttelot, at the time of his death, believed Stanley to be dead owing to the absence of news, none having been received since the rumours brought by deserters.

Tippoo Tib was described as overwhelmed by the death of Major Barttelot, and declared to the officers at the Falls that he would have given half his fortune to prevent the catastrophe.

Mr. Stanley had addressed the following letters, *en route*, to his unfortunate second in command, but they were never destined to reach the Major's hands, as we have seen. A pathetic interest now attaches to these remarkable communications, which afford a striking illustration of the shrewd "grip" of Stanley's mind, and of his marvellous attention to details and jealous care for the welfare of all under his command, whether whites or blacks.

The pests of Central Africa, the Arab slave-hunters, were the cause of the non-delivery of these letters, and it was solely due to the slavers on the Aruwimi that the reserve force, after passing months of anxiety, amounting at times to despair, at the Yambuya fort, set out, without a word of direction as to road, transport, and attitude of natives, upon that brave enterprise of rescue which ended in the murder of the Major some hours beyond Nurenia.

"CAMP ON S. BANK, ARUWIMI RIVER
(OPPOSITE ARAB SETTLEMENT),
"*September 18th*, 1887.

"MY DEAR MAJOR,—You will, I am certain, be as glad to get news—definite and clear—of our movements as I am to feel that I have at last an opportunity of presenting them to you. As they will be of immense comfort to you and your assistants and followers, I shall confine myself to giving you the needful details. We have travelled three hundred and forty English miles, to make only one hundred and ninety-two geographical miles of our easterly course. This has been performed in eighty-three days, which gives us a rate of four and one-tenth miles per day. We have yet to make one hundred and thirty geographical miles, or a winding course, perhaps, of two hundred and thirty miles, which, at the same rate of march as hitherto, we may make in fifty-five days. We started from Yambuya three hundred and eighty-nine souls, whites and blacks. We have now three hundred and thirty-three, of whom fifty-six are so sick that we are obliged to leave them behind us at this Arab camp of Ugarrowwa. We are fifty-six men short of the number with which we left Yambuya. Of these, thirty men have died—four from poisoned arrows, six left in the bush or speared by the natives—twenty-six have deserted *en route*, thinking that they would be able to follow a caravan of Manyuema, which we met following the river downwards. But this caravan, instead of going on, returned to this place, and our deserters, misled by this, will probably follow our track downwards until they meet you, or are exterminated by the natives. Be not deluded by any statements they may make. Were I to send men to you, I, of course, would send you a note; but in no instance a verbal message, or any message at all by the scum of the camp. Should you meet them, you will have to secure them thoroughly.

"The first day we left you we made a good march, which terminated in a fight, the foolish natives firing their own village as they fled. Since that day we have had, probably, thirty fights. The first view of us the natives had inspired them to show fight. As far as Panga Falls we did not lose a man or meet with any serious obstacles to navigation. Panga is a big cataract, with a decided fall. We cut a road round it on the south bank, and dragged our canoes and went on again.

"We had intended to follow a native path, which would take us toward our destination, with the usual windings of the road. For ten days we searched for a road, and then took an elephant track, which led us into an interminable forest, totally uninhabited. Fearing to lose ourselves altogether, we cut a road to the river, and have followed the river ever since. From the point where we struck the river to Mugwye's country—four days' journey below Panga—we fared very well. Food was abundant; we made long marches, and no halts whatever. Beyond Mugwye's up to Engweddeh was a wilderness, eleven days' march, villages being inland, and mostly foodless. From this date our strength declined rapidly. People were lost in the bush as they searched for food, or were slain by the natives. Ulcers, dysentery, and grievous sickness, ending in fatal debility, attacked the people.

Hence our enormous loss since leaving Panga—thirty dead and twenty-six deserters. Besides which, we are obliged to leave fifty-six behind, so used up that, without a long rest, they would also die. Of the Somalis, one is dead (Achmet); the other five are at this camp until our return from the Lake. Of the Soudanese, one is dead; we leave three behind to-day. All the whites are in perfect condition to-day—thinnish, but with plenty of go.

"Among our fights we have had over fifty wounded, but they all recovered except four. Stairs was severely wounded with an arrow, which penetrated an inch and a half within a little below the heart, in the left breast. He is all right now.

"We have had one man shot dead by some person unknown in the camp; another was shot in the foot, resulting in amputation. This latter case, now in a fair state of health, we leave behind to-day. The number of hours we have marched ought to have taken us back to you by this time, but we had to daily hew our path through forest and jungle to keep along the river, because the river banks were populated. The forest inland contains no settlements that we know or have heard of. By means of canoes, we were able to help the caravan, carry the sick and several loads. The boat helped us immensely. Were I to do the work over again, I should collect canoes as large as possible, man them with sufficient paddlers, and load up with goods and sick. On the river between Yambuya and Mugwye's country the canoes are numeous, and tolerably large. The misfortune is that the Zanzibaris are exceedingly poor boatmen. In my force there are only about fifty who can paddle or pull an oar; but even these have saved our caravan immense labour, and many lives which otherwise would have been sacrificed.

"Our plan has been to paddle from one rapid to another. On reaching strong water, or shoals, we have unloaded canoes and poled or dragged them up with long rattan or other creepers through the rapids, then loaded up again and pursued our way until we met another obstacle. The want of sufficient and proper food regularly pulls people down very fast, and they have not that strength to carry the loads which has distinguished them while with one in other parts of Africa. Therefore, any means to lighten the labour of the caravan is commendable.

"If Tippoo Tib's people have not yet joined you, I do not expect you will be very far from Yambuya. You can make two journeys by river for one that you can do on land. Slow as we have been coming up, and cutting our way through, I shall come down river like lightning. The river will be a friend indeed, for the current alone will take us 20 miles a day, and I will pick up as many canoes as possible to help us on our second journey up river. Follow the river closely, and do not lose sight of our track. When the caravan which takes this passes you, look out for your men, or they will run in a body, taking valuable goods with them.

"Give my best salaams and kind remembrances from us all to your fellows. Bid them cheer up: so many miles a day will take you here in so many days. It depends on your own going, and your power, how many or how few you will be.

"I need not say that I wish you the best of health and luck and good fortune, because you are a part of myself; therefore, good-bye.

"Yours very truly,

"(Signed) HENRY M. STANLEY.

"Major Barttelot."

Written in pencil on the first corner of the above is the following:—

"Dear Major,—I send this on to you—the former attempt was a failure.—W. E. STAIRS."

"FORT BODO, IBWIRI DISTRICT,
"*February* 14*th*, 1888.

"MY DEAR MAJOR,—After much deliberation with my officers upon the expediency of the act, I have resolved to send twenty couriers to you with this letter, which I know will be welcome to you and your comrades, as the briefest note, or even word, from you would be to us.

"Fort Bodo is 120 English miles from Kavalli, on the Albert Nyanza, or 77 hours of caravan marching (west), and is almost on the same latitude. It is 527 English miles almost direct east from Yambuya, or 352 hours of caravan marching. You can easily find out where it is by tracing on your map a straight line from Yambuya to Kavalli, and dividing that line into five equal parts: four-fifths would be the distance from Yambuya, and one-fifth from our post on the Nyanza. I send a little tracing of our route, sufficiently exact for your use, and on it I have marked the principal places where food may be had between Yambuya and the Nyanza.

"First, Mugwye's villages on north bank of river, 184 English miles, or 124 hours' caravan marching from Yambuya. The villages are five in number, backed by extensive cultivations of manico, bananas, and Indian corn.

"Second, Aveysheba villages, 59 English miles, or 36 hours' marching. These villages are on south bank, near a lazy creek 35 yards wide. There were five villages here when we passed, and abundance of very large bananas. Ten miles higher up on north bank there is a settlement close to river, untouched by us. It is situate at the foot of a rapid. By sending forty guns across river from Aveysheba you would gain better access to these.

"Third, confluence of the Nepoko with the Aruwimi, villages on south bank, opposite the big cataract of the Nepoko, which tumbles into the Aruwimi in fine view of landing place. Nepoko is almost as large as the Aruwimi, therefore you cannot mistake it. We found abundance at these villages, which are numerous and scattered. They are situate 39 miles above Aveysheba, or 26 hours' caravan marching.

"Fourth is Ugarrowwa's, an Arab settlement on north bank. Hospitality would be given, but food would be dear, and you would have to disburse cloth. It is 93 miles above the last place, or 62 hours' marching.

"Fifth, Fort Bodo is a place built by us in Ibwiri after our return from the Albert Nyanza

We have abundance of food here. To-day our stock inside the fort consists of four cows and a calf, ten goats (three of these being milk goats), six tons of Indian corn. Outside the fort we have four acres planted in corn and half-an-acre of beans. We have bananas for two miles west of us, and half-a-mile on either side of the fort. Our houses are comfortable, whitewashed within and without; the men mostly sleek and glossy. Stairs, Nelson, Parke, and Williams are with me here. Jephson is out foraging for live stock, and I hope to see him to-morrow. Our force consists of 184 present, 11 at Ipolo, 56 at Ugarrowwa's—total rank and file, 251 souls. By the new road we estimate Fort Bodo to be distant from Ugarrowwa's 162 English miles, or 108 hours' marching for caravan.

"Sixth is the brow of the plateau looking down on the Albert Nyanza, and between it and Fort Bodo we have experienced no want of provisions of all kinds necessary. The object of this letter is not only to encourage and cheer you and your people up with definite and exact information of your whereabouts and the land ahead of you, but to save you from a terrible wilderness whence we all narrowly escaped with our lives. I wrote you from Ugarrowwa's a letter sufficiently detailed to enable you to understand what our experience was between Yambuya and Ugarrowwa's; therefore, I begin from Ugarrowwa's and go east to the Nyanza.

"After leaving Ugarrowwa's on the 19th September, we had 285 souls with us, and 56 sick at Ugarrowwa's—total 341. By October 6th we had travelled along south bank of river, amidst a country depopulated and devastated by Arabs, and our condition was such, from a constant pinching want, that we had 8 deaths and 52 sick—that is, 60 utterly used up in sixteen days. I was forced to leave Captain Nelson, lamed by ulcers, and 52 sick, and 82 loads with him, at a camp near the river, while we would explore ahead, find provisions, and send back relief.

"Until 18th October we marched in the hope of obtaining food, and on this day we entered a settlement of Manyuema, but in the interval we had travelled through uninhabited forest, where we lived on wild fruit and fungi. In these twelve days we had lost 22 by desertion and death, but the condition of the survivors was terrible. We were all emaciated and haggard, but the majority were mere skeletons. On the 29th, Nelson's party was relieved, but out of 52 there were only 5 left. Many had died, many had deserted, about 20 were out foraging, out of which party ultimately only 10 turned up.

"On the 28th October we marched from the Manyuema settlement for this place, Ibwiri. Here we found such an abundance that we halted to recuperate until November 24. On this day the advance column mustered as follows:—

Sick at Ugarrowwa's (Arab settlement) ..	56
Sick at Manyuema settlement	38
Present in Ibwiri	174
Total	268

On September 19 we numbered	341
On November 24	268
Dead and missing	73

"Beyond this place, I believe no Arab or Manyuema had ever penetrated; consequently we suffer no scarcity, and on November 24 we marched from Ibwiri for the Albert Lake, which we reached December 13, having lost only one by death, the result of wilderness miseries, and we returned to this place from the Albert Lake, January 7, having lost only four, two of whom died from cause of wilderness miseries; one, Klamis Kaururu (chief), inflammation of the lungs; one, Ramaque Vin Kuru, fever and ague, contracted near Lake. Thus, between November 24 and January 7, we had lost but 5; 3 of these deaths were the result of privations undergone in the wilderness.

"We first met the Manyuema on the last day of August, and parted from them January 6th. In the interval we have lost 118 through death and desertion. In their camps it was as bad as in the wilderness, for they ground us down by extortion so extreme that we were naked in a short time. They tempted the Zanzibaris to sell their rifles and ammunition, ramrods, officers' blankets, &c., and then gave food so sparingly that these crimes were of no avail. Finally, besides starving them, tempting them to ruin the Expedition, they speared them, scourged them, and tied them up, until in one case death ended his miseries. Never were such abject slaves of slaves as our people had become under the influence of the Manyuema. Yet, withal, they preferred death by scourging, spearing, starvation, ill-treatment, to the duty of load-bearing and marching on to happier regions. Out of 38 men left at the Manyuema camp, 11 had died, 11 others may turn up, but it is doubtful. However, we have only received 16—16 out of 38! Comment is unnecessary.

"When we left the Manyuema camp, October 28th, we were obliged to leave our boat and 70 loads behind, as it was absolutely impossible to carry them. Parke and Nelson were detailed to look after them. We hoped that we should find some tree out of which we could make a sizeable canoe, or buy or seize one ready-made. Arriving at the Nyanza, we found neither tree nor canoe, therefore were obliged to retrace our steps here quickly, to send men back to the Manyuema settlement for the boat and loads. The boat and 37 loads were brought here by Stairs, and nearly 100 men, the day before yesterday.

"You will understand, then, that Emin Pasha not being found or relieved by us, made it as much necessary that we should devote ourselves to this work, as it was imperative when we set out, June 28, 1887, from Yambuya. And you will also understand how anxious we are all about you. We dread your inexperience and your want of influence with your people. If, with me, people preferred the society of the Manyuema blackguards to me, who am known to them for twenty years, how much more so with you, a stranger to them and their language? Therefore the cords of anxiety are strained to exceeding tension. I am pulled east to Emin Pacha and drawn west to you, your comrades, people, and goods.

"Nearly eight months have elapsed, and perhaps you have not had a word from us, though I wrote a long letter from Ugarrowwa's. We were to have been back by December—it is now

February, and no one can conjecture how far you may have reached. Did the *Stanley* arrive in due time? Did she arrive at all? Did Tippoo Tib join you? Are you alone with your party, or is Tippoo Tib with you? If the latter, why so slow that we have not a word? If alone, we understand that you are very far from us? These are questions daily agitating us.

Therefore we are agreed that while we bear the boat to the Albert Nyanza, to make a final finish with Emin Pasha, we should try to communicate with you. With that view, I have called for volunteers at £10 per head reward to bear this letter to you even as far as Yambuya, if (as it might chance, for all we know to the contrary) you have not started, and to return to me with your news. To us, who have gone over the ground, Yambuya seems about a month's distance only. Stairs escorts the twenty as far as Ugarrowwa's, and brings to me the fifty-six men, who are all recovered (as we hear). Stairs on his return will find me about five days from the Lake, and we will then push on fast to the Lake, when he has joined us.

According to my calculation, we shall be on the Lake April 10th; all about Emin Pasha will be settled by April 25th; on the 13th May we shall be back here; on the 29th we shall be at Ugarrowwa's, if we have not met you. We shall surely, I hope, meet with the return messengers. *Re* these messengers, I should advise your keeping two of them as guides—Ruga-Rugu in front; but they should be free of loads. Send the eighteen and two others back to me as soon as you can, because the sooner we hear from you, the sooner we will join hands; and after settling the Emin Pasha question, we shall have only one anxiety, which will be to get you safely up here.

"Assuming that Tippoo Tib's people are with you, our guides (two) will bring you quickly on here, and we shall probably meet here or at Ugarrowwa's; and, the *Stanley* steamer arrived within reasonable time, you have arrived at some place about twenty-two or twenty-four of our former journeys from Yambuya, below Mugwye's, as I take it. Hence, before you get near the Arab influence, where your column will surely break up if you are alone, I order you to go to the nearest place (Mugwye's, Aveysheba, or Nepoko confluence) that is to you, and there to build a strong camp and wait us; but, whatever you decide upon, let me know. If you come near Ugarrowwa's you will lose men, rifles, powder, everything of value; your own boys will betray you, because they will sell food so dearly that your people, from stress of hunger, will steal everything.

"At either of the three places above, you will get safety and food until we relieve you. So long as you are stationary there is no fear of desertion—but the daily task, added to constant insufficiency of food, will sap the fidelity of your best men. (These directions are only in case of you being alone, without Arab aid. If Tippoo Tib's people are with you, I presume you are coming along slowly.)

"With everybody's best wishes to you, I send my earnest prayer that you are, despite all unwholesome and evil conjectures, where you ought to be, and that this letter will reach you in time to save you from that forest misery and from the fangs of the ruthless Manyuema blackguards. To every one of your officers also these good wishes are given, from

"Yours most sincerely,

(Signed) "HENRY M. STANLEY.

"To Major Barttelot, Commanding Rear Column, E.P.R.E."

The Major, who was the second son of Sir Walter Barttelot, M.P., was an officer in the 1st Battalion of the Royal Fusiliers. He served with distinction in the Afghan campaign, for which he received the medal and clasp, and in the Egyptian campaign, winning a similar decoration. He was born in March, 1859, and had therefore only reached his twenty-ninth year when he unhappily fell a victim to the fears and cowardice of his Manyuema guards.

The leave-taking of the two brave men at Yambuya was, after all, their final parting. The letter in which Mr. Stanley conferred the command of the rear column upon his trusted associate contained a warm tribute to the personal qualities of his subordinate, and his confidence in him was not misplaced. Major Barttelot was "faithful unto death," and no nobler tribute can grace a hero's tomb.

CHAPTER XII.

MID-TROPICAL AFRICA.

THE Victorian era will always be remembered as the Golden Age of African discovery. At the beginning of the century the knowledge of the civilized world as to the physical phenomena and native races of the Dark Continent was less accurate than it was two thousand years ago. But during the past fifty years a blaze of light has been thrown across the vast peninsula from ocean to ocean, and the work of the explorer, as far as inner Africa is concerned, is well-nigh finished. The character of the interior, its products, and its peoples have been for ages the subjects of frequent and earnest disputation amongst the *savants* of ancient and modern Europe. At length the veil of mystery which has enshrouded the mighty continent for well-nigh twenty centuries has been lifted, and many old-time notions as to the hydrology, and population, and productions of what was supposed to be a vast desert waste have been ruthlessly dispelled by the researches of Schweinfurth, Thomson, De Brazza, Cameron, Speke, Burton, Livingstone, Stanley, Baker, and others. One by one the blanks in the maps of our school days have been filled up, and the broad yellow patch which served for the Central African desert has given place to that wonderful lacustrine system of fresh water seas and mighty rivers, with their thousand affluents, the discovery of which has proved the greatest geographical feat of this or any generation, and the crowning glory of modern scientific exploration. The great African mystery is being cleared up with almost dramatic swiftness and fulness, and we have every reason to believe that when Mr. Stanley once more emerges into the light of day, from the Great Congo basin, he will bring with him the solution of the few remaining problems connected with that region which are at present unsettled, and which have exercised the minds and intellects of thoughtful men from the days of the Ptolemies down to the present era. Mr. Stanley claims already to have added a population of fifty millions to the sum total of the known peoples of the world by his own discoveries in Equatorial Africa alone. He has in years past drawn aside the curtain and made known to us the existence of

" myriads of dusky nations, hidden for long ages altogether out of sight and knowledge, on the fertile plains and uplands of the head-waters of the Zambesi, the Lualabu, and Old Nile," and as the first white traveller to traverse the stretch of unknown forest land between the Congo and the Albert Nyanza, his report to the Royal Geographical Society of his successful enterprise in crossing this virgin land, and so leaving only one considerable blank remaining on the map of the continent, is of surpassing interest.

His letter, read to the Society on April 9th, 1889, describing his adventures and discoveries during his perilous journey through a zone of cannibalism and savagery probably unmatched on the face of the globe, is a most remarkable narrative, and affords a fresh illustration of the qualities of endurance, the resolution and the courage of Stanley, whose name will be inseparably linked with the continent which he has pierced through and through—the Columbus of its ocean-like expanses of plain and thicket and bosky woodland—bestowing by his genius and devotion a new world upon commerce and civilisation. The horrors of the Congo Forest are set forth in such clear and graphic language that we can now see, in a measure, something of the real nature of the struggle against nature which this heroic man has been waging, out of sight, in the African wilderness for close upon two years. In his letter the great explorer gives an account of the new land lately traversed by his force, and now about to be retraversed by them. Yambuya, their entrenched camp, is in N. lat. 1.17, E. long. 25.8, and the objective point of their expedition was Karalli, N. lat. 1.22, E. long. 30.30, the distance in a direct line being 322 geographical miles. This region was previously unexplored by either white or Arab. The force numbered 389 rank and file. They bore a steel boat 28 feet by 6 feet with them, about three tons of ammunition, and a couple of tons of provisions and sundries. With all these goods and baggage they had a reserve force of about 180 supernumeraries; half of them carried, besides their Winchesters, billhooks to pierce the bush and cut down obstructions.

After describing the impediments to their progress and the close, stagnant, gloomy region of the primeval forest, Mr. Stanley describes the tactics of the natives. Every art known to native minds for annoying strangers was practised by them. The path frequently had shallow pits, filled with sharpened splinters or skewers, deftly covered over with large leaves. For barefooted people this was terrible. Often the skewers would perforate the feet quite through, and at other times the tops would be buried in the feet, resulting in gangrenous sores. "One of the approaches to every village was a straight road, perhaps a 100 yards long and 12 feet wide, cleared of jungle, but bristling with these skewers carefully and cunningly hidden at every place likely to be trodden by an incautious foot. The real path was crooked, and took a wide detour, the cut road appeared so tempting, so straight, and so short. At the village end was the watchman, to beat his drum and sound the alarm, when every native would take his weapons and proceed to the appointed place to ply his bow at every opportunity. Yet despite a formidable list of hostile measures and attempts no life was lost, though our wounded increased in number."

After a few days of this work the path became an elephant track leading south-east and south-south-west. They again changed their course to the north-east and east, and by the 5th July touched the river again. "The river," continues Mr. Stanley "retained a noble width—from 500 to 900 yards, with an island here and there, sometimes a group of islets, the resorts of oyster-fishermen. Such piles of oyster-shells! On one island I measured a heap 30 paces long, 12 feet wide at the base, and 4 feet high. At almost every bend of the river, generally in the middle of the bend—because a view of the river approach up and down stream may be had—there is a village of cone huts—of the candle-extinguisher type. Some bends have a large series of these villages populated by some thousands of natives. The villages of the Banalya, Bakubana, and Bungangeta tribes run close to each other along a single long bend. The first has become famous through the tragedy ending in the death of Major Barttelot. An island opposite the site of the Bungangeta villages I occupied to reorganize the Expedition, which had almost become a wreck through the misfortunes of the rear column. The abundance found by us will never be found again, for the Arabs have followed my track by hundreds, and destroyed villages and plantations, and what the Arabs spare the elephant herds complete."

"One of the most serious features in the opposition of the natives was the fact that they were armed with poisoned arrows. At Avisibba, about half-way between Panga Falls and the Nepoko, the natives attacked our camp in quite a resolute and determined fashion. Their stores of poisoned arrows they thought gave them every advantage; and, indeed, when the poison is fresh it is most deadly. Lieutenant Stairs and five men were wounded by these. Lieutenant Stairs's wound was from an arrow the poison of which was dry—it must have been put on some days before. After three weeks or so, he recovered strength, though the wound was not closed for months. One man received a slight puncture near the wrist; another received a puncture near the shoulder in the muscles of the arm; one was wounded in the gullet—tetanus ended the sufferings of all. We were much exercised as to what this poison might be that was so deadly."

"On returning from the Nyanza to relieve the rear column, under Major Barttelot, we halted at Avisibba, and, rummaging among the huts, found several packets of dried red ants or pismires. It was then we knew that the dried bodies of these, ground into powder, cooked in palm oil, and smeared over the wooden points of the arrows, was the deadly irritant by which we lost so many fine men with such terrible suffering. The large black ant, whose bite causes a great blister, would be still more venomous prepared in the same way; the bloated spiders, an inch in length, which are covered with prickles most painful to the touch, would form another terrible compound, the effects of which make one shudder to think of."

This is Mr. Stanley's description of the

Aruwimi:—"The Aruwimi has many names—the Dudu, Biyerre, Huali, the Nevva, Nowelle, Itiri—for the last 300 miles of its course, but upward to its source it has a singular, wide-spreading fame under the name of Ituri. The aborigines of the Nyanza—the open plateau and forest tribes down to within a few miles of the Nepoko—all unite in calling it the Ituri."

Summing up, the writer says:—"I look upon the country lying between the Albert Nyanza and the lake discovered by me in 1876 as promising curious revelations. Up to this moment I am not certain to which river the last lake belongs, whether to the Nile or to the Congo. I believe to the latter, but what I am sure of is that it has no connection with the Albert Nyanza. The Ruwenzori slopes must supply a large portion of the waters of the Semliki river; the plateau south-west and west must supply the rest. But it is at the water-parting between the Semliki and some other river south or south-west that real interest begins."

Here and there it appears that the young forest growing on the site of some long abandoned clearing was so dense that the pioneers had actually to hew a tunnel through the luxuriant vegetation. Morning and evening were dark and gloomy, and a dun sombre shade was over all things, and a silence prevailed which was at times painful to bear. But with the bursting forth of the sun's rays from behind the clouds at mid-day the whole forest was once more roused to life. Clouds of beautiful insects swept through the tremulous air, or shot athwart the shafts of golden sunshine which struck down through the tangled boughs overhead. Butterflies, moths, and many-hued birds gleamed and fluttered in the glittering light, and the Congo Forest seemed to be a veritable paradise for the enthusiastic entomologist.

Insects of all forms and sorts were to be seen, from the most beautiful and harmless to the most hideous and deadly. It will be noticed that Mr. Stanley traced the death-dealing poison of the fatal arrow-tips used by the tribes along the Aruwimi to a preparation made from dried red ants. The end of the letter contains a sentence which will eventually prove full of meaning. Mr. Stanley speaks of the great prolific area of riverine territory lying to the south of the Albert Lake, towards the mysterious Muta Nzige—the Nyanza from whose banks he turned reluctantly away in 1876, when just about to launch the *Lady Alice* upon its unknown waters. In this region, which, from its Alpine aspect, Stanley named the Switzerland of Africa, stands Mount

Gordon Bennett, with its towering peaks wrapped in wreaths of perpetual snow, and its rugged flanks scored and ploughed by foaming torrents that rush down headlong through the fissures of the torn and rugged rocks to the Lake at its foot. The sentence—"a shoulder of the western wall prevented us from verifying the connection of the Muta Nzige with the Congo or with the Nile—I am certain it does not connect with the Albert Nyanza—and this must be left till we take our journey homeward"—shows that it is the evident intention of Stanley to clear up the mystery of this region (if possible) before coming home to England. It is interesting to know that this letter to the Royal Geographical Society contains a curious confirmation of a story related by Herodotus as to the existence of dwarfs in Central Africa. "Between the Nepoko and the grass land the dwarfs are exceedingly numerous," says Mr. Stanley. "They are called Wambutti. The Pasha's people with us recognised in them the Tikki-tikki farther north. I suppose we saw about 150 villages of camps of the Wambutti. They are a very venomous, cowardly, and thievish race." In Herodotus, II. 32-33, we find a story told by Etearchus, King of the Ammonians, to some men of Cyrene, and by them to Herodotus, to the effect that certain adventurous Nasamones, wishing to discover the source of the Nile—the problem of the ages—made a long and painful journey into the interior of the Libyan country beyond the desert. After passing through a region infested by wild beasts, and a tract of sandy sterile waste, they came at last to trees growing in a plain—the forest belt—and while engaged in plucking the fruit growing thereon, they were attacked and captured by "small men, less than the ordinary size," who carried them away through a vast expanse of marshes until they came to a town the inhabitants of which were all of the same diminutive size. By the town flowed a river containing crocodiles, which river Etearchus conjectured to be the Nile—a belief to which Herodotus also inclines. The story has, no doubt, some little historical value, and it is also interesting as showing that nearly 3,000 years ago the difficulties attending the exploration of the inner heart of the African continent were much the same as they are to-day.

CHAPTER XIII.

EMIN "FAITHFUL" STILL.

AS it was always part of Mr. Stanley's plan to return to Europe eventually *viâ* the east coast and Zanzibar, he now decided to go back to the Aruwimi and bring forward his rear column to the Albert Nyanza, and then, having re-united his forces, to strike due east for the Indian Ocean. The Pasha still demurred to leaving his people. "Would it be right," he asked, "to abandon them to their fate? Would it not be consigning them to certain ruin? Disputes would arise, factions would be formed. I should have to leave them their arms and ammunition. The more ambitious would aspire to be chiefs by force. From these rivalries would spring hate and mutual slaughter, until none of them were left, that is, supposing the Egyptian irregulars after all refused to follow me out of the province, or supposing any of them (even a remnant) remained behind."

Leaving Mr. Jephson, some Soudanese, and a party of Zanzibaris in the care of Emin, Stanley set out from the neighbourhood of the Lake for the return journey westward, on the 25th of May, taking with him 111 Zanzibaris, and 101 of Emin's people, to act as porters, in the place of the men who had died or deserted. He was now daily getting more and more anxious for some news of the rear column under Major Barttelot, of which he had heard no tidings whatever since he left the Aruwimi, in June, 1887. The journey to the Congo was comparatively uneventful. The column was in good marching order. The ground was covered, without any casualties of consequence, by rapid marches in 82 days. The journey to the Albert Nyanza had taken from June 28th to December 12th, with a loss of some hundreds of lives.

On the road the couriers sent out months before to find the Major were overtaken, sorely scarred with wounds, and reduced by death, and on the 17th of August Mr. Stanley reached Banalya, a stockaded fort on the Aruwimi, without gleaning any news of the rear column anywhere on the entire route from the Lakes to the Congo. As the head of the Expedition drew up to the fort he saw a white man, who turned out to be Mr. Bonny.

"Well, my dear Bonny," said the Commander somewhat anxiously, "where is the Major?"

"He is dead, sir; shot by the Manyuema about a month ago," replied Mr. Bonny.

"Good God. And Mr. Jamieson?"

"He is gone to Stanley Falls, to try and get some more men from Tippoo Tib." (Mr. Jamieson died of fever some time after this, on his way down the Congo.)

"And Mr. Troup?"

"Mr. Troup has gone home, sir, invalided."

"Hem! Well, where is Ward?"

"Mr. Ward is at Bangala, sir."

"Heavens alive! Then you are the only one here."

"Yes, sir."

Disaster had fallen upon the unfortunate rear column. In fact, it was a total wreck. Out of 257 men there were only 71 remaining; out of the 71 only 52, on mustering them, seemed fit for service, and these mostly were scarecrows.

On the 5th of September Mr. Stanley was once more on his way to the Albert Nyanza. In the interval strange rumours have reached the outer world through Egypt and the Soudan. In August last the Governor of the Equatorial Province is said to have defeated a strong body of troops sent against him by the present Mahdi, to have become master of the whole region south of Bahr-el-Ghazel, and to have been accompanied in a vigorous and triumphant campaign by "several white officers." As Mr. Stanley and all his surviving officers and forces have now been back in the Province of the Equator for several months, if all has gone on well, as Stanley anticipated, this report is not unlikely true. When Emin parted with the Expedition, for the time, on the Albert Nyanza, in May, 1888, he was quite well, and full of resolution to pursue the advantages he had already gained. He was known to have "ivory in abundance, cattle by thousands, and sheep and food of all kinds in such abundance that he was able to relieve the Relief Expedition," and "to give numbers of things," said Stanley, "to all our white and black men."

We have, therefore, every reason to hope that the courage, and energy, and resource which have accomplished so much in the past may be relied upon for much more.

The magnificent enterprise which was organized for the succour of the illustrious Pasha, it is true, has been completely successful, but only at the cost of a dreadful sacrifice of life. This was, from the nature of the case, however, well-nigh inevitable. But though the venture has met with some misfortunes, it has attained the purposes for which it was organized. It has succoured Emin and his faithful garrisons, and the matchless intrepidity and the gallant heroism displayed by its leader and his companions in the most romantic deed of daring of modern times, have earned for all concerned in the undertaking the esteem and gratitude of the entire civilized world.

The story of the Emin Pasha Relief Expedition supplies us not only with a stirring tale of adventure, but with an entirely new chapter of African geography. It is interesting to notice that the idea of reaching the Lake Province from the Congo, and of thus linking together the two great arteries through which the life-blood of civilization is destined to flow into the heart of Africa, was first of all conceived by General Gordon, and that the hero we all lament was on the point of undertaking this task when he was sent to Khartoum for the last time. Mr. Stanley has carried out the idea. He has shown how nearly the two great waterways of the continent are related, and how their sources of supply overlap. Others will find easier ways still to the Albert Nyanza from the Congo, probably somewhat to the north of Mr. Stanley's route. But the first comer always has the hardest task, and the problem, in the main, is solved. Of Emin—the Faithful One—we may, when we remember and recall all we have heard of him, be fully persuaded that he will not leave his Province or his post unless either his toil is hopeless, or (what is not altogether improbable) his task is so far accomplished that he has placed the Pearl of the Soudan, once Egyptian, completely beyond the grasp of the tottering despotism of Khartoum. Africa has of late years furnished some significant triumphs to civilization and science and humanity. These triumphs have been won by the steady, self-sacrificing devotion of such men as Livingstone, Gordon, Cameron, Baker, Thomson, Stanley, and Emin, whose chief aim has been directed, with a remarkable unanimity, disinterestedness, and far-sightedness, to the protection of the native races from their worst enemy—the Arab slave-trader.

PRINTED BY J. S. VIRTUE AND CO., LIMITED, CITY ROAD, LONDON.

LIST OF WORKS

PUBLISHED BY

J. S. VIRTUE & CO., LIMITED,

26, IVY LANE, LONDON.

Architecture, The Amateur's Guide to. By S. SOPHIA BEALE, Author of "The Louvre." With several hundred Illustrations. Cloth gilt, 3s. 6d.

"Admirably adapted to fill the position it assumes. It explains, in the simplest possible manner, the distinctions not only between the various styles of architecture, but between the different styles of ornamentation; and in every case there is a small illustration which cannot fail to fix in the mind the distinctions of which the authoress has been talking."—*Scotsman.*

Art as Applied to Dress. By Miss L. HIGGIN, late of the Royal School of Art Needlework, South Kensington, with Special Reference to Harmonious Colouring. Royal 16mo, cloth, 2s. 6d.

"We hail this prettily got up little volume because its contents are at once practical and suggestive."—*The Queen.*

"Treated in an exhaustive, but not tedious manner . . . worthy of careful study by every woman . . . exquisitely printed."—*Lady's Pictorial.*

Blunt's (Rev. J. J.) Sketch of the Reformation in England. With an Introductory Chapter by the Rev. CUNNINGHAM GEIKIE, D.D., Author of the "Life and Words of Christ." New Edition. With 16 full-page Illustrations. Fcap. 8vo, cloth gilt, 2s. 6d.

Breakfast Dishes for every Morning in Three Months. By Miss M. L. Allen. Tenth Edition, cloth boards, silver gilt, 1s. 6d.; Paper, 1s.

"The question 'What shall we have for Breakfast?' is here answered in a practical way."—*The Queen.*

"Supplies a long-felt want by housekeepers"—*Graphic.*

Bunyan's (John) Pilgrim's Progress. With 8 full-page Illustrations. Crown 8vo, cloth, gilt edges, 3s. 6d.

Christian Birthday Souvenir, The. Selected and arranged by "DELTA." Imperial 16mo, cloth gilt, gilt edges, 2s. 6d.

"This is a Birthday Album, but not of the usual kind. . . . The poetical quotations have been collected with considerable care and spiritual taste."—*The Sword and Trowel.*

"A beautiful Birthday Text Book."—*The Baptist.*

"This is the best 'Birthday' record we have seen."—*Primitive Methodist.*

"An excellent Birthday Book."—*The Rock.*

Christian Year, The. By the Rev. THOMAS KEBLE. Thoughts in Verse for the Sundays and Holy Days throughout the Year. New and attractive Edition. Printed in colours, with specially designed Borders. Crown 8vo, cloth gilt, gilt gilt edges, 2s. 6d.

Cutts' (E. L.) Scenes and Characters of the Middle Ages. By the Rev. Edward L. Cutts, late Hon. Sec. of the Essex Archæological Society. With 182 Engravings on Wood. 8vo, cloth gilt, 7s. 6d.

Contents:—The Monks of the Middle Ages—The Hermits and Recluses of the Middle Ages—The Pilgrims of the Middle Ages—The Secular Clergy of the Middle Ages—The Minstrels of the Middle Ages—The Knights of the Middle Ages—The Merchants of the Middle Ages.

"A series of valuable papers. . . . A lucid text, terse and full of matter, excellently assists the illustrations, which of themselves would be a welcome boon to the antiquarian."—*Daily Telegraph.*

"The illustrations alone, taken as they are from some old rare manuscripts and other trustworthy sources, would make this volume extremely valuable."—*Morning Post.*

Decorative Composition, A Manual of, for Designers, Decorators, Architects, and Industrial Artists. By Henri Mayeux. Translated by J. Gonino, and Illustrated by nearly 300 Engravings. Post 8vo, 6s.

Dee, The River. Its Aspect and History. By the late Dean Howson. Revised to date, with New Preface and Appendix on the Salmon Fisheries by Alfred Rimmer. New Edition, with 93 Engravings on Wood. Fcap. 4to, cloth gilt, gilt edges, 7s. 6d.

"A very acceptable gift book. . . . The volume is a very pretty and interesting souvenir of both the Dee and the Dean, the paper, printing, and binding being worthy of the subject and its treatment."—*Liverpool Courier.*

"This is a new edition of an interesting work, of which the worst that could be said was that there was not enough of it."—*The Weekly Albion.*

"It would be difficult to find a more suitable Christmas gift book for those who live along the banks of the Dee to send to their friends at a distance than the beautiful illustrated description of that river."—*Liverpool Mercury.*

"A charming book, a worthy memorial of the late Dean Howson. . . . Mr. Rimmer's best work is in the beautiful drawings reproduced on wood with which the volume is enriched."—*Southport Guardian.*

Economical French Cookery for Ladies. Adapted to English Households by A Cordon Bleu. Cloth, silver gilt, 1s. 6d.; paper, 1s.

"The lectures are very interesting, containing many receipts for delicious soups and dishes."—*Liverpool Courier.*

Emin Pasha, The Life and Work of, in Equatorial Africa. By the Rev. Henry W. Little, Author of "Madagascar: Its History and People," "How to Save Egypt," &c., &c. With Portrait, and Map of the Stanley Route. Crown 8vo, price 2s. 6d.

Famous Books. By W. Davenport Adams. Sketches in the Highways and Byways of English Literature. More's "Utopia," The First English Tragedy and Comedy, Ascham's "Schoolmaster," Sidney's "Arcadia," &c., &c. New Edition, with Illustrations, attractive binding, cloth gilt, gilt edges, 3s. 6d.

Foxe's Book of Martyrs. Being a History of Christian Martyrdom from the Earliest Times. Carefully Revised by the Rev. M. Crombie, M.A. With eight full-page Illustrations. Crown 8vo, cloth gilt, gilt edges, 3s. 6d.

Glimpses of the Land of Scott. By David Hannay. Illustrated by J. MacWhirter, A.R.A. Handsomely bound, cloth gilt, gilt edges, 10s. 6d.

"The volume is a model of careful printing. . . . Readers of Scott must be satisfied by his knowledge of the poet and his country, and the tourist will find his impressions of the borderland full of interest, and his suggestions as to walking trips a real service."—*Saturday Review.*

"Mr. MacWhirter may be congratulated on a happy selection, and most of his drawings are admirably suggestive of the scenery."—*The Times.*

"Mr. MacWhirter's cuts are sometimes charming, and nearly always excellent."—*Athenæum.*

"No more agreeable guide could be wished for either in Edinburgh, in the Lammermuir region, along the Tweed, or on the Border."—*Glasgow Herald.*

"The illustrations are charming, some of them being perfect gems."—*The Standard.*

Great Historic Families of Scotland (The). By JAMES TAYLOR, M.A., D.D., F.S.A.Scot., Author of the "Pictorial History of Scotland." New and cheaper Edition, in two vols., royal 8vo, £1 1s.

"It is no bare genealogical record. It does not contain a dry page or a mouldy paragraph. . . . Much of it is as readable as the 'Tales of a Grandfather'. . . . Dr. Taylor has produced a work of great value."—*The Scotsman.*

"Dr. Taylor has accomplished a useful task. . . . To a great number of Scotsmen this work should prove welcome, and it has a really valuable feature in its elaborate index."—*Athenæum.*

"No book of the kind has appeared to be compared with it for importance and value to the historical student. It is, indeed, a remarkably interesting record." —*The Daily Telegraph.*

Hack's (Maria) Stories from English History during the Middle Ages. Revised by DAVID MURRAY SMITH, Author of "Tales of Chivalry and Romance," &c. With Eight full-page Illustrations. Crown 8vo, cloth gilt, gilt edges, 3s. 6d.

Invalid Cookery, with Instructions on the Preparation of Food for the Sick. By MARY DAVIES. Cloth, silver gilt, 1s. 6d. Paper, 1s.

"One of the best and completest invalid cookeries that we have seen." *Saturday Review.*

Italy; its Rivers, its Lakes, its Cities, its Arts. With nearly 170 Illustrations. Small Quarto, cloth gilt, gilt edges, 15s.

"Amply illustrated with 164 woodcuts, many of them of full-page size and well engraved . . . not only forms a most useful companion for travellers to the Sunny South, but well deserves a prominent place in a lady's library, on her drawing-room table, and amongst her Christmas presents."—*The Queen.*

Jerusalem, the Holy City. By Colonel Sir Charles Wilson. With about 80 Engravings in Steel and Wood. Small Imperial 4to. Cloth gilt, gilt edges, £1 1s.

"No work we know gives so good an idea of the Holy City with its sacred surroundings and its historical remains."—*Times.*

"From every point of view it is a book which deserves high commendation."
Guardian.

Lacroix's The Arts in the Middle Ages, and at the Period of the Renaissance. By Paul Lacroix, Curator of the Imperial Library of the Arsenal, Paris. Edited and revised by Walter Armstrong, M.A. Illustrated with 12 Chromo-lithographic Prints by F. Kellerhoven, and upwards of 400 Engravings on Wood. Imperial 8vo, £1 1s.

"One of the most interesting and instructive guides to a delightful kind of knowledge."—*Illustrated London News.*

"An exceptionally fine reissue. The work is as comprehensive in design as it is beautiful in finish, externally and internally."—*Glasgow Herald.*

Men who have Risen. A Book for Boys. Including the graphic stories of the rise of the Peel Family, and the struggles of such men as Hugh Miller, Wilson the Ornithologist, Smeaton the Engineer, and Robert Stephenson. With Eight full-page Illustrations. Crown 8vo, cloth gilt, gilt edges, 3s. 6d.

Nurses' Companion in the Sick Room. By Mary Davies. Cloth, silver gilt, 1s. 6d.; paper, 1s.

"Excellent little book."—*Morning Post.*

"Gives plain instructions for relief in the early cases of sickness, or simple treatment for small ailments."—*Queen.*

One Hundred and One Methods of Cooking Poultry. With Hints on Selection, Trussing, and Carving. By Aunt Chloe. Price 1s.; or cloth, silver gilt, 1s. 6d.

"A very useful and handy cookery guide, and one that is much wanted and will be much appreciated."—*Spectator.*

Rhine (The); from its Source to the Sea. By KARL STIELER and others. Profusely illustrated with nearly 170 Illustrations. Small 4to, cloth gilt, gilt edges, 15s.

"The book is a very attractive one."—*Glasgow Herald.*

Riviera (The), both Eastern and Western. By HUGH MACMILLAN, D.D. 24 page Illustrations, and nearly 150 in the text, including descriptions and Illustrations of the following towns, among many others:—Nice, Cannes, Mentone, San Remo, &c. &c. Cloth gilt, gilt edges, £1 1s.

"Many books have been written about the Riviera, but none are so full of information and pleasant reading and so picturesquely illustrated as that just published."—*The Queen.*

Rome, the Eternal City; its Church Monuments, Art, and Antiquities. By FRANCIS WEY. Profusely illustrated with nearly 300 Illustrations. Small 4to, cloth gilt, gilt edges, 15s.

"It is much to be recommended. It gives almost a perfect idea of the Eternal City on the seven hills as it has been revolutionized by municipal Haussmannizing and swept by new brooms."—*The Times.*

Savouries and Sweets. Seventh Edition, cloth, silver gilt, 1s. 6d.; paper, 1s.

"Of great merit."—*Saturday Review.*

"More useful than many of its more pretentious rivals."—*The Lady.*

"So very adequate is this manual in its way that its cost will be begrudged by but comparatively few householders."—*Western Daily Mercury.*

Shakespere (William) Works of. Edited by CHARLES KNIGHT. With upwards of 1,000 Illustrations. New library edition, in 8 vols. 8vo, cloth gilt, red top, per volume, 6s.

Shelmerdine's (W.) Psalms and other Portions of Scripture, marked for Chanting. Small 8vo, cloth cut flush, price 1s.

Signification and Principles of Art. By C. H. Waterhouse. A Critical Essay for general readers, being an attempt to determine the essential nature of the Fine Arts, and to distinguish them from other modes of human activity. New edition, 2s. 6d.

"We have no hesitation in warmly commending Mr. Waterhouse's deeply-thoughtful and very interesting essay."—*Graphic.*

"The essay has much in it that is new and interesting. It forms a valuable contribution to the discussion of the principles of taste."—*The Scotsman.*

Sound Investments for Small Savings. By George B. Baker. Small 8vo, price 1s.; cloth, 1s. 6d.

Switzerland; its Mountains, Valleys, Lakes, and Rivers. Illustrated by A. Closz with nearly 170 Drawings. Small 4to, cloth gilt, gilt edges, 15s.

"Capital descriptions of the alpine roads and passes, the lakes of East Switzerland and of the Western Lakes."—*Volunteer Service Gazette.*

Women of Worth. A Book for Boys and Girls. With full-page Illustrations by W. Dickes. Crown 8vo, cloth gilt, gilt edges, 3s. 6d.

Wood's (Rev. J. G.) Nature's Teachings, Human Invention anticipated by Nature. By the Author of "Homes without Hands," &c., &c., with 300 Illustrations. New Edition. Demy 8vo, cloth gilt, 7s. 6d.

"Of very high interest even to those who care but little for natural history as a study."—*Standard.*

"Certainly no more thoroughly instructive volume could be made a gift of than this one."—*Leeds Mercury.*

Man and Beast, Here and Hereafter. Fifth Edition, 6s.

"The book is delightful."—*British Quarterly Review.*

"Filled with anecdotes which are very entertaining."—*Saturday Review.*

"Extremely readable and interesting."—*Pall Mall Gazette.*

"We recommend all lovers of natural history to read it."—*Land and Water.*

Louisa de la Ramé

A Dog of Flanders

A Christmas Story

Louisa de la Ramé

A Dog of Flanders
A Christmas Story

ISBN/EAN: 9783743427693

Manufactured in Europe, USA, Canada, Australia, Japa

Cover: Foto ©Andreas Hilbeck / pixelio.de

Manufactured and distributed by brebook publishing software
(www.brebook.com)

Louisa de la Ramé

A Dog of Flanders

DESCENT FROM THE CROSS—RUBENS

A DOG OF FLANDERS

A Christmas Story

BY

LOUISA DE LA RAMÉ

("OUIDA")

ILLUSTRATED

BOSTON

JOSEPH KNIGHT COMPANY

PUBLISHERS

LIST OF ILLUSTRATIONS.

A DOG OF FLANDERS:

A STORY OF NOEL.

NELLO and Patrasche were left all alone in the world.

They were friends in a friendship closer than brotherhood. Nello was a little Ardennois; Patrasche was a big Fleming. They were both of the same age by length of years, yet one was still young, and the other was already old. They had dwelt together almost all their days: both were orphaned and destitute, and owed their lives to the same hand. It had been the beginning of the tie between them, their first bond of sympathy; and it had strengthened day by day, and had grown with their growth, firm and indissoluble, until they loved one another very greatly.

Their home was a little hut on the edge of a little village — a Flemish village a league from Antwerp, set amidst flat breadths of pasture and corn-lands, with long lines of poplars and of alders bending in the breeze on the edge of the great

canal which ran through it. It had about a score of houses and homesteads, with shutters of bright green or sky-blue, and roofs rose-red or black and white, and walls whitewashed until they shone in the sun like snow. In the centre of the village stood a windmill, placed on a little moss-grown slope: it was a landmark to all the level country round. It had once

been painted scarlet, sails and all, but that had been in its infancy, half a century or more earlier, when it had ground wheat for the soldiers of Napoleon; and it was now a ruddy brown, tanned by wind and weather. It went queerly by fits and starts, as though rheumatic and stiff in the joints from age, but it served the whole neighborhood, which

would have thought it almost as impious to carry grain elsewhere as to attend any other religious service than the mass that was performed at the altar of the little old gray church, with its conical steeple, which stood opposite to it, and whose single bell rang morning, noon and night with that strange, subdued, hollow sadness which every bell that hangs in the Low Countries seems to gain as an integral part of its melody.

Within sound of the little melancholy clock, almost from their birth upward, they had dwelt together, Nello and Patrasche, in the little hut on the edge of the village, with the cathedral spire of Antwerp rising in the northeast, beyond the great green plain of seeding grass and spreading corn

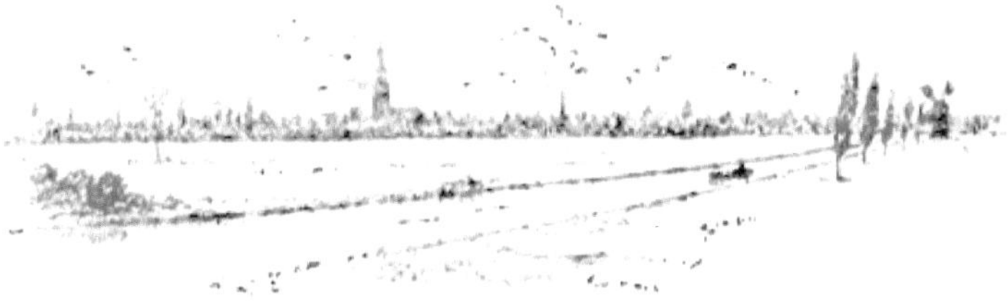

that stretched away from them like a tide-less, changeless sea. It was the hut of a very old man, of a very poor man — of old Jehan Daas, who in his time had been a soldier, and who remembered the wars that had trampled the country as oxen tread down the furrows, and who had brought from his service nothing except a wound, which had made him a cripple.

When old Jehan Daas had reached his full eighty, his daughter had died in the

Ardennes, hard by Stavelot, and had left him in legacy her two-year old son. The old man could ill contrive to support himself, but he took up the additional burden uncomplainingly, and it soon became welcome and precious to him. Little Nello — which was but a pet diminutive for Nicolas — throve with him, and the old man and the little child lived in the poor little hut contentedly.

It was a very humble little mud-hut indeed, but it was clean and white as a sea-shell, and stood in a small plot of garden-ground that yielded beans and herbs and pumpkins. They were very poor, terribly poor — many a day they had nothing at all to eat. They never by any chance had enough: to have had enough to eat would have been to have reached paradise at once. But the old man was very gentle and good to the boy, and the boy was a beautiful, innocent, truthful, tender-natured creature; and they

were happy on a crust and a few leaves of cabbage, and asked no more of earth or Heaven; save indeed that Patrasche should be always with them, since without Patrasche, where would they have been?

For Patrasche was their alpha and omega; their treasury and granary; their store of gold and wand of wealth; their bread-winner and minister; their only friend and comforter. Patrasche dead or gone from them, they must have laid themselves down and died likewise. Patrasche was body, brains, hands, head and feet to both of them: Patrasche was their very life, their very soul. For Jehan Daas was old and a cripple, and Nello was but a child; and Patrasche was their dog.

A dog of Flanders — yellow of hide, large of head and limb, with wolf-like ears that stood erect, and legs bowed and feet widened in the muscular development wrought in his breed by many generations of hard service. Patrasche came of

a race which had toiled hard and cruelly from sire to son in Flanders many a century — slaves of slaves, dogs of the people, beasts of the shafts and the harness, creatures that lived straining their sinews in the gall of the cart, and died breaking their hearts on the flints of the streets.

Patrasche had been born of parents who had labored hard all their days over the sharp-set stones of the various cities and the long, shadowless, weary roads of the two Flanders and of Brabant. He had been born to no other heritage than those of pain and of toil. He had been fed on curses and baptized with blows. Why not? It was a Christian country, and Patrasche was but a dog. Before he was fully grown he had known the bitter gall of the cart and the collar. Before he had entered his thirteenth month he had become the property of a hardware dealer, who was accustomed to wander over the land north and south, from the blue sea to the green mountains. They sold him for a small price because he was so young.

This man was a drunkard and a brute. The life of Patrasche was a life of hell. To deal the tortures of hell on the animal creation is a way which the Christians have of showing their belief in it. His purchaser was a sullen, ill-living, brutal Brabantois, who heaped his cart full with pots and pans and flagons and buckets, and other wares of crockery and brass and tin, and left Patrasche to draw the load as best he might, whilst he himself lounged idly by the side in fat and sluggish ease, smoking his black pipe and stopping at every wine-shop or café on the road.

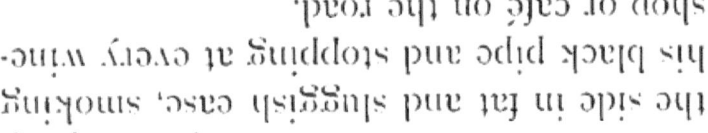

Happily for Patrasche — or unhappily — he was very strong: he came of an iron race, long born and bred to such cruel travail; so that he did not die, but managed to drag on a wretched existence under the brutal burdens, the scarifying lashes, the hunger, the thirst, the blows, the curses and the exhaustion which are

the only wages with which the Flemings repay the most patient and laborious of all their four-footed victims. One day, after two years of this long and deadly agony, Patrasche was going on as usual along one of the straight, dusty, unlovely roads that lead to the city of Rubens. It was full midsummer, and very warm. His cart was very heavy, piled high with goods in metal and in earthenware. His owner sauntered on without noticing him otherwise than by the crack of the

whip as it curled round his quivering loins. The Brabantois had paused to drink beer himself at every wayside house, but he had forbidden Patrasche to stop a moment for a draught from the canal. Going along thus, in the full sun, on a scorching high-

way, having eaten nothing for twenty-four hours, and, which was far worse to him, not having tasted water for nearly twelve, being blind with dust, sore with blows and stupefied with the merciless weight which dragged upon his loins, Patrasche, for once, staggered and foamed a little at the mouth, and fell.

He fell in the middle of the white, dusty road, in the full glare of the sun: he was sick unto death, and motionless. His master gave him the only medicine in his pharmacy — kicks and oaths and blows with a cudgel of oak, which had been often the only food and drink, the only wage and reward, ever offered to him. But Patrasche was beyond the reach of any torture or of any curses. Patrasche lay, dead to all appearances, down in the white powder of the summer dust. After a while, finding it useless to assail his ribs with punishment and his ears with maledictions, the Brabantois — deeming life gone in him, or going so nearly that his carcass was forever use-

less, unless indeed some one should strip it of the skin for gloves — cursed him

fiercely in farewell, struck off the leathern bands of the harness, kicked his body heavily aside into the grass, and, groaning

and muttering in savage wrath, pushed the cart lazily along the road up hill, and left the dying dog there for the ants to sting and for the crows to pick.

It was the last day before Kermesse, away at Louvain, and the Brabantois was in haste to reach the fair and get a good place for his truck of brass wares. He was in fierce wrath, because Patrasche had been a strong and much-enduring animal, and because he himself had now the hard task of pushing his charette all the way to Louvain. But to stay to look after Patrasche never entered his thoughts: the beast was dying and useless, and he would steal, to replace him, the first large dog that he found wandering alone out of sight of its master. Patrasche had cost him nothing, or next to nothing, and for two long, cruel years he had made him toil ceaselessly in his service from sunrise to sunset, through summer and winter, in fair weather and foul.

He had got a fair use and a good profit out of Patrasche: being human, he was

wise, and left the dog to draw his last breath alone in the ditch, and have his bloodshot eyes plucked out as they might be by the birds, whilst he himself went on his way to beg and to steal, to eat and to drink, to dance and to sing, in the mirth at Louvain. A dying dog, a dog of the cart — why should he waste hours over its agonies at peril of losing a handful of copper coins, at peril of a shout of laughter?

Patrasche lay there, flung in the grass-green ditch. It was a busy road that day, and hundreds of people, on foot and on mules, in wagons or in carts, went by, tramping quickly and joyously on to Louvain. Some saw him, most did not even look: all passed on. A dead dog more or less — it was nothing in Brabant: it would be nothing anywhere in the world.

After a time, amongst the holiday-makers, there came a little old man who was bent and lame, and very feeble. He was in no guise for feasting: he was very poorly and miserably clad, and he

dragged his silent way slowly through the dust amongst the pleasure-seekers. He looked at Patrasche, paused, wondered, turned aside, then kneeled down in the rank grass and weeds of the ditch, and surveyed the dog with kindly eyes of pity.

There was with him a little rosy, fair-haired, dark-eyed child of a few years old, who pattered in amidst the bushes, that were for him breast-high, and stood gazing with a pretty seriousness upon the poor great, quiet beast.

Thus it was that these two first met — the little Nello and the big Patrasche.

The upshot of that day was, that old Jehan Daas, with much laborious effort, drew the sufferer homeward to his own little hut, which was a stone's throw off amidst the fields, and there tended him with so much care that the sickness, which had been a brain-seizure, brought on by heat and thirst and exhaustion, with time and shade and rest passed away, and health and strength returned, and Patrasche staggered up again upon his four stout, tawny legs.

Now for many weeks he had been useless, powerless, sore, near to death; but all this time he had heard no rough word, had felt no harsh touch, but only the pitying murmurs of the little child's voice and the soothing caress of the old man's hand.

In his sickness they too had grown to care for him, this lonely old man and the little happy child. He had a corner of the hut, with a heap of dry grass for his bed; and they had learned to listen eagerly for his breathing in the dark night, to tell them that he lived; and

when he first was well enough to essay a loud, hollow, broken bay, they laughed aloud, and almost wept together for joy at such a sign of his sure restoration; and little Nello, in delighted glee, hung

round his rugged neck with chains of marguerites, and kissed him with fresh and ruddy lips.

So then, when Patrasche arose, himself again, strong, big, gaunt, powerful, his great wistful eyes had a gentle astonishment in them that there were no curses to rouse him and no blows to drive him;

and his heart awakened to a mighty love, which never wavered once in its fidelity whilst life abode with him.

But Patrasche, being a dog, was grateful. Patrasche lay pondering long with grave, tender, musing brown eyes, watching the movements of his friends.

Now, the old soldier, Jehan Daas, could do nothing for his living but limp about a little with a small cart, with which he carried daily the milk-cans of those happier neighbors who owned cattle away into the town of Antwerp. The villagers gave him the employment a little out of charity — more because it suited them well to send their milk into the town by so honest a carrier, and bide at home themselves to look after their gardens, their cows, their poultry or their little fields. But it was becoming hard work for the old man. He was eighty-three, and Antwerp was a good league off, or more.

Patrasche watched the milk-cans come and go that one day when he had got well and was lying in the sun with the

wreath of marguerites round his tawny neck.

The next morning, Patrasche, before the old man had touched the cart, arose and walked to it and placed himself betwixt

its handles, and testified as plainly as dumb show could do his desire and his ability to work in return for the bread of charity that he had eaten. Jehan Daas resisted long, for the old man was one of those who thought it a foul shame to bind dogs to labor for which Nature never

formed them. But Patrasche would not be gainsaid: finding they did not harness him, he tried to draw the cart onward with his teeth.

At length Jehan Daas gave way, vanquished by the persistence and the gratitude of this creature whom he had succored. He fashioned his cart so that Patrasche could run in it, and this he did every morning of his life thenceforward.

When the winter came, Jehan Daas thanked the blessed fortune that had brought him to the dying dog in the ditch that fair-day of Louvain; for he was very old, and he grew feebler with each year, and he would ill have known how to pull his load of milk-cans over the snows and through the deep ruts in the mud if it had not been for the strength and the industry of the animal he had befriended. As for Patrasche, it seemed heaven to him. After the frightful burdens that his old master had compelled him to strain under, at the call of the

whip at every step, it seemed nothing to him but amusement to step out with this little light green cart, with its bright brass cans, by the side of the gentle old man who always paid him with a tender caress and with a kindly word. Besides, his work

was over by three or four in the day, and after that time he was free to do as he would — to stretch himself, to sleep in the sun, to wander in the fields, to romp with the young child or to play with his fellow-dogs. Patrasche was very happy.

Fortunately for his peace, his former owner was killed in a drunken brawl at

the kermesse of Mechlin, and so sought not after him nor disturbed him in his new and well-loved home.

A few years later, old Jehan Daas, who had always been a cripple, became so par-

alyzed with rheumatism that it was impossible for him to go out with the cart any more. Then little Nello, being now grown to his sixth year of age, and knowing the town well from having accompanied his grandfather so many times, took his place

beside the cart, and sold the milk and received the coins in exchange, and brought them back to their respective owners with a pretty grace and seriousness which charmed all who beheld him.

The little Ardennois was a beautiful child, with dark, grave, tender eyes, and a lovely bloom upon his face, and fair locks that clustered to his throat; and many an artist sketched the group as it went by him — the green cart with the brass flagons of Teniers and Mieris and Van Tal, and the great, tawny-colored, massive dog, with his belled harness that chimed cheerily as he went, and the small figure that ran beside him, which had little white feet in great wooden shoes, and a soft, grave, innocent, happy face like the little fair children of Rubens.

Nello and Patrasche did the work so well and so joyfully together that Jehan Daas himself, when the summer came and he was better again, had no need to stir out, but could sit in the doorway in the sun and see them go forth through the

garden wicket, and then doze and dream and pray a little, and then awake again as the clock tolled three, and watch for their return. And on their return Patrasche would shake himself free of his harness with a bay of glee, and Nello would recount with pride the doings of the day; and they would all go in together to their meal of rye bread and milk or soup, and would see the shadows lengthen over the great plain, and see the twilight veil the fair cathedral spire; and then lie down together to sleep peacefully while the old man said a prayer.

So the days and the years went on, and the lives of Nello and Patrasche were happy, innocent and healthful.

In the spring and summer especially were they glad. Flanders is not a lovely land, and around the burgh of Rubens it is perhaps least lovely of all. Corn and colza, pasture and plough, succeed each other on the characterless plain in wearying repetition, and, save by some gaunt gray tower, with its peal of pathetic bells,

or some figure coming athwart the fields, made picturesque by a gleaner's bundle or a woodman's fagot, there is no change, no

variety, no beauty anywhere; and he who has dwelt upon the mountains or amidst the forests feels oppressed as by imprisonment with the tedium and the endlessness of that vast and dreary level. But it is green and very fertile, and it has wide horizons that have a certain charm of their own even in their dulness and monotony; and amongst the rushes by the water-side the flowers grow and the trees rise tall and fresh where the barges glide with their great hulks black against the sun, and their little green barrels and vari-colored flags gay against the leaves. Anyway, there is greenery and breadth of space enough to be as good as beauty to a child and a dog; and these

two asked no better, when their work was done, than to lie buried in the lush grasses on the side of the canal, and watch the cumbrous vessels drifting by and bringing the crisp salt smell of the sea amongst the blossoming scents of the country summer.

True, in the winter it was harder, and they had to rise in the darkness and the bitter cold, and they had seldom as much as they could have eaten any day, and the hut was scarce better than a shed when the nights were cold, although it looked so pretty in warm weather, buried in a great kindly-clambering vine, that never bore fruit, indeed, but which covered it with luxuriant green tracery all through the months of blossom and harvest. In winter the winds found many holes in the walls of the poor little hut, and the vine was black and leafless, and

the bare lands looked very bleak and drear without, and sometimes within the floor was flooded and then frozen. In winter it was hard, and the snow numbed the little white limbs of Nello, and the icicles cut the brave, untiring feet of Patrasche.

But even then they were never heard to lament, either of them. The child's wooden shoes and the dog's four legs would trot manfully together over the frozen fields to the chime of the bells on the harness; and then sometimes, in the streets of Antwerp, some housewife would bring them a bowl of soup and a handful of bread, or some kindly trader would throw some billets of fuel into the little cart as it went homeward, or some woman in their own village would bid them keep some share of the milk they carried for their own food; and then they would run over the white lands, through the early darkness, bright and happy, and burst with a shout of joy into their home.

So, on the whole, it was well with them,

very well; and Patrasche, meeting on the highway or in the public streets the many dogs who toiled from daybreak into nightfall, paid only with blows and curses, and

loosened from the shafts with a kick to starve and freeze as best they might,—Patrasche in his heart was very grateful to his fate, and thought it the fairest and the kindliest the world could hold. Though

he was often very hungry indeed when he lay down at night; though he had to work in the heats of summer noons and the rasping chills of winter dawns; though his feet were often tender with wounds from the sharp edges of the jagged pavement; though he had to perform tasks beyond his strength and against his nature, —yet he was grateful and content: he did his duty with each day, and the eyes that he loved smiled down on him. It was sufficient for Patrasche.

There was only one thing which caused Patrasche any uneasiness in his life, and it was this. Antwerp, as all the world knows, is full at every turn of old piles of stones, dark and ancient and majestic, standing in crooked courts, jammed against gateways and taverns, rising by the water's edge, with bells ringing above them in the air, and ever and again out of their arched doors a swell of music pealing. There they remain, the grand old sanctuaries of the past, shut in amidst the squalor, the hurry, the crowds, the unloveliness and the

commerce of the modern world, and all day long the clouds drift and the birds circle and the winds sigh around them, and beneath the earth at their feet there sleeps — RUBENS.

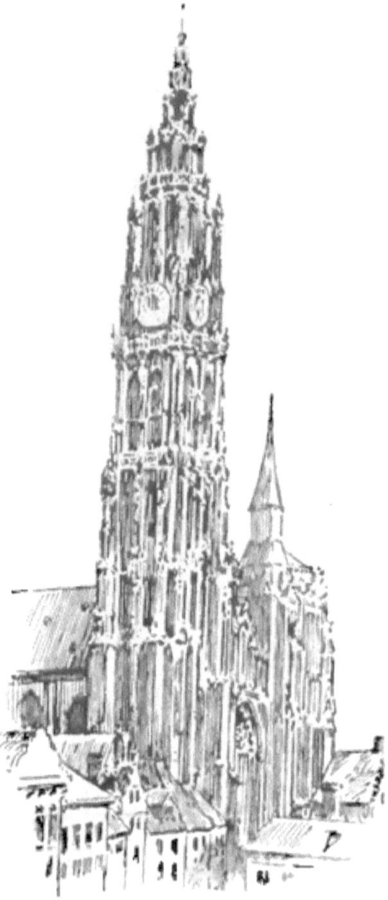

And the greatness of the mighty Master still rests upon Antwerp, and wherever we turn in its narrow streets his glory lies therein, so that all mean things are thereby transfigured; and as we pace slowly through the winding ways, and by the edge of the stagnant water, and through the noisome

courts, his spirit abides with us, and the heroic beauty of his visions is about us, and the stones that once felt his footsteps and bore his shadow seem to arise and speak of him with living voices. For the city which is the tomb of Rubens still lives to us through him, and him alone.

It is so quiet there by that great white sepulchre — so quiet, save only when the organ peals and the choir cries aloud the Salve Regina or the Kyrie Eleison. Sure no artist ever had a greater gravestone than that pure marble sanctuary gives to him in the heart of his birthplace in the chancel of St. Jacques.

Without Rubens, what were Antwerp? A dirty, dusky, bustling mart which no man would ever care to look upon save the traders who do business on its wharves. With Rubens, to the whole world of men it is a sacred name, a sacred soil, a Bethlehem where a god of Art saw light, a Golgotha where a god of Art lies dead.

O nations! closely should you treasure your great men, for by them alone will

the future know of you. Flanders in her generations has been wise. In his life she glorified this greatest of her sons, and in his death she magnifies his name. But her wisdom is very rare.

Now, the trouble of Patrasche was this. Into these great, sad piles of stones, that reared their melancholy majesty above the crowded roofs, the child Nello would many and many a time enter, and disappear through their dark, arched portals, whilst Patrasche, left without upon the pavement, would wearily and vainly ponder on what could be the charm which thus allured from him his inseparable and beloved companion. Once or twice he did essay to see for himself, clattering up the steps with his milk-cart behind him; but thereon he had been always sent back again summarily by a tall custodian in black clothes and silver chains of office; and fearful of bringing his little master into trouble, he desisted, and remained couched patiently before the churches until such time as the boy reappeared. It was not the fact of his going

into them which disturbed Patrasche: he knew that people went to church: all the village went to the small, tumbledown, gray pile opposite the red windmill. What troubled him was that little Nello always looked strangely when he came out, always very flushed or very pale; and whenever he returned home after such visitations would sit silent and dreaming, not caring to play, but gazing out at the evening skies beyond the line of the canal, very subdued and almost sad.

What was it? wondered Patrasche. He thought it could not be good or natural for the little lad to be so grave, and in his dumb fashion he tried all he could to keep Nello by him in the sunny fields or in the busy market-place. But to the churches Nello would go: most often of all would he go to the great cathedral; and Patrasche, left without on the stones by the iron fragments of Quentin Matsys' gate, would stretch himself and yawn and sigh, and

even howl now and then, all in vain, until the doors closed, and the child perforce came forth again, and winding his arms about the dog's neck would kiss him on his

broad, tawny-colored forehead, and murmur always the same words: "If I could only see them, Patrasche! — if I could only see them!"

What were they? pondered Patrasche,

looking up with large, wistful, sympathetic eyes.

One day, when the custodian was out of the way and the doors left ajar, he got in for a moment after his little friend and saw. "They" were two great covered pictures on either side of the choir.

Nello was kneeling, rapt as in an ecstasy, before the altar-picture of the Assumption, and when he noticed Patrasche, and rose and drew the dog gently out into the air, his face was wet with tears, and he looked up at the veiled places as he passed them, and murmured to his companion, "It is so terrible not to see them, Patrasche, just because one is poor and cannot pay! He never meant that the poor should not see them when he painted them, I am sure. He would have had us see them any day, every day: that I am sure. And they keep them shrouded there—shrouded in the dark, the beautiful things!—and they never feel the light, and no eyes look on them, unless rich people come and pay. If I could only see them, I would be content to die."

But he could not see them, and Patrasche could not help him, for to gain the silver piece that the church exacts as the price for looking on the glories of the Elevation of the Cross and the Descent of the Cross was a thing as utterly beyond the powers of either of them as it would have been to scale the heights of the cathedral spire. They had never so much as a sou to spare: if they cleared enough to get a little wood for the stove, a little broth for the pot, it was the utmost they could do. And yet the heart of the child was set in sore and endless longing upon beholding the greatness of the two veiled Rubens.

The whole soul of the little Ardennois thrilled and stirred with an absorbing passion for Art. Going on his ways through the old city in the early days before the sun or the people had risen, Nello, who looked only a little peasant-boy, with a great dog drawing milk to sell from door to door, was in a heaven of dreams whereof Rubens was the god. Nello, cold and hungry, with stockingless feet in wooden shoes,

and the winter winds blowing amongst his curls and lifting his poor thin garments, was in a rapture of meditation, wherein all that he saw was the beautiful fair face

of the Mary of the Assumption, with the waves of her golden hair lying upon her shoulders, and the light of an eternal sun shining down upon her brow. Nello, reared in poverty, and buffeted by fortune, and untaught in letters, and unheeded by men, had the compensation or the curse which is called Genius.

No one knew it. He as little as any. No one knew it. Only indeed Patrasche, who, being with him always, saw him draw with chalk upon the stones any and every thing that grew or breathed, heard him on his little bed of hay murmur all manner of timid, pathetic prayers to the spirit of the great Master; watched his gaze darken and his face radiate at the evening glow of sunset or the rosy rising of the dawn; and felt many and many a time the tears of a strange, nameless pain and joy, mingled together, fall hotly from the bright young eyes upon his own wrinkled, yellow forehead.

"I should go to my grave quite content if I thought, Nello, that when thou

growest a man thou couldst own this hut and the little plot of ground, and labor for thyself, and be called Baas by thy neighbors," said the old man Jehan many an hour from his bed. For to own a bit of soil, and to be called Baas — master — by the hamlet round, is to have achieved the highest ideal of a Flemish peasant; and the old soldier, who had wandered over all the earth in his youth, and had brought nothing back, deemed in his old age that to live and die on one spot in contented humility was the fairest fate he could desire for his darling. But Nello said nothing.

The same leaven was working in him that in other times begat Rubens and Jordaens and the Van Eycks, and all their wondrous tribe, and in times more recent begat in the green country of the Ardennes, where the Meuse washes the old walls of Dijon, the great artist of the Patroclus, whose genius is too near us for us aright to measure its divinity.

Nello dreamed of other things in the

future than of tilling the little rood of earth, and living under the wattle roof, and being called Baas by neighbors a little poorer or a little less poor than himself. The cathedral spire, where it rose beyond the fields in the ruddy evening skies or in the dim, gray, misty mornings, said other things to him than this. But these he told only to Patrasche, whispering, childlike, his fancies in the dog's ear when they went together at their work through the fogs of the daybreak, or lay together at their rest amongst the rustling rushes by the water's side.

For such dreams are not easily shaped into speech to awake the slow sympathies of human auditors; and they would only have sorely perplexed and troubled the poor old man bedridden in his corner, who, for his part, whenever he had trodden the streets of Antwerp, had thought the daub of blue and red that they called a Madonna, on the walls of the wine-shop where he drank his sou's worth of black beer, quite as good as any of the famous

altar-pieces for which the stranger folk traveled far and wide into Flanders from every land on which the good sun shone.

There was only one other beside Patrasche to whom Nello could talk at all of his daring fantasies. This other was little Alois, who lived at the old red mill on the grassy mound, and whose father, the miller, was the best-to-do husbandman in all the village. Little Alois was only a pretty baby with soft round, rosy features, made lovely by those sweet dark eyes that the Spanish rule has left in so many a Flemish face, in testimony of the Alvan dominion, as Spanish art has left broadsown throughout the country majestic palaces and stately courts, gilded house-fronts and sculptured lintels — histories in blazonry and poems in stone.

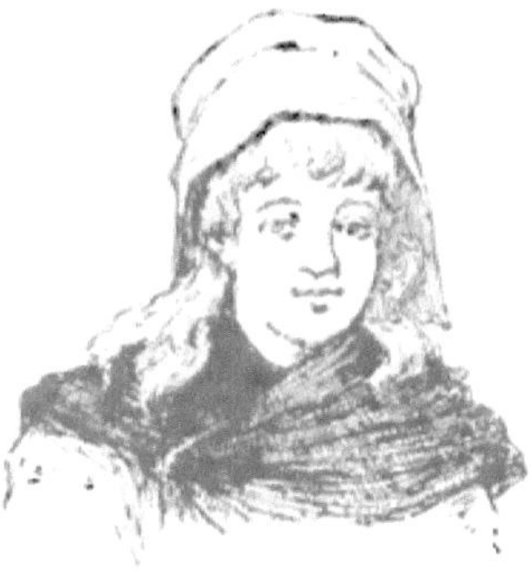

Little Alois was often with Nello and Patrasche. They played in the fields, they ran in the snow, they gathered the daisies

and bilberries, they went up to the old gray church together, and they often sat together by the broad wood-fire in the mill-house. Little Alois, indeed, was the richest child in the hamlet. She had neither brother nor sister; her blue serge dress had never a hole in it; at kermesse she had as many gilded nuts and Agni Dei in sugar as her hands could hold; and when she went up for her first communion her flaxen curls were covered with a cap of richest Mechlin lace, which had been her mother's and her grandmother's before it came to her. Men spoke already, though she had but twelve years, of the good wife she would be for their sons to woo and win; but she herself was a little gay, simple child, in nowise conscious of her heritage, and she loved no playfellows so well as Jehan Daas' grandson and his dog.

One day her father, Baas Cogez, a good man, but somewhat stern, came on a pretty group in the long meadow behind the mill,

where the aftermath had that day been cut. It was his little daughter sitting amidst the hay, with the great tawny head of Patrasche on her lap, and many wreaths

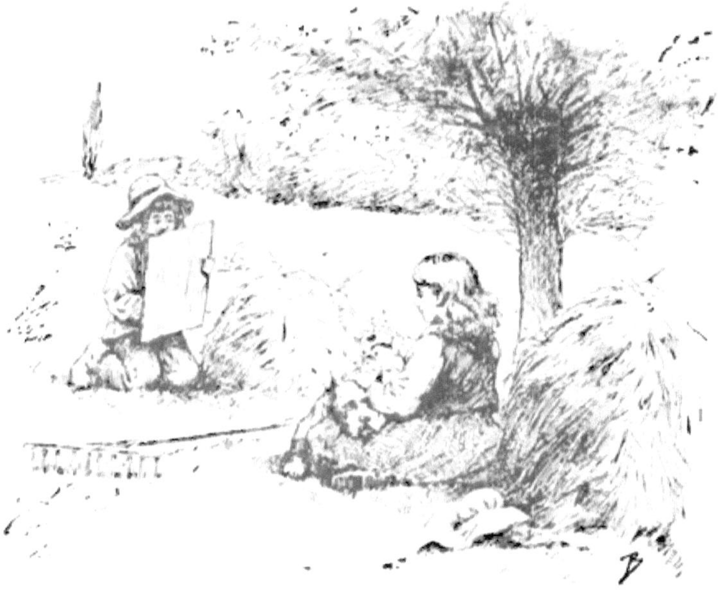

of poppies and blue cornflowers round them both: on a clean smooth slab of pine wood the boy Nello drew their likeness with a stick of charcoal.

The miller stood and looked at the portrait with tears in his eyes, it was so

strangely like, and he loved his only child closely and well. Then he roughly chid the little girl for idling there whilst her mother needed her within, and sent her indoors crying and afraid: then, turning, he snatched the wood from Nello's hands. "Dost do much of such folly?" he asked, but there was a tremble in his voice.

Nello colored and hung his head. "I draw everything I see," he murmured.

The miller was silent: then he stretched his hand out with a franc in it. "It is folly, as I say, and evil waste of time: nevertheless, it is like Alois, and will please the house-mother. Take this silver bit for it and leave it for me."

The color died out of the face of the young Ardennois: he lifted his head and put his hands behind his back. "Keep your money and the portrait both, Baas Cogez," he said simply. "You have been often good to me." Then he called Patrasche to him, and walked away across the fields.

"I could have seen them with that

franc," he murmured to Patrasche, "but I could not sell her picture — not even for them."

Baas Cogez went into his mill-house sore troubled in his mind. "That lad must not be so much with Alois," he said to his wife that night. "Trouble may come of it hereafter: he is fifteen now, and she is twelve; and the boy is comely of face and form."

"And he is a good lad and a loyal," said the housewife, feasting her eyes on the piece of pine wood where it was throned above the chimney with a cuckoo clock in oak and a Calvary in wax.

"Yea, I do not gainsay that," said the miller, draining his pewter flagon.

"Then, if what you think of were ever to come to pass," said the wife, hesitatingly, "would it matter so much? She will have enough for both, and one cannot be better than happy."

"You are a woman, and therefore a

fool," said the miller harshly, striking his pipe on the table. "The lad is naught but a beggar, and, with these painter's fancies, worse than a beggar. Have a care that they are not together in the future, or I will send the child to the surer keeping of the nuns of the Sacred Heart."

The poor mother was terrified, and promised humbly to do his will. Not that she could bring herself altogether to separate the child from her favorite play-mate, nor did the miller even desire that extreme of cruelty to a young lad who was guilty of nothing except poverty. But there were many ways in which little Alois was kept away from her chosen compan-ion; and Nello being a boy proud and quiet and sensitive, was quickly wounded, and ceased to turn his own steps and those of Patrasche, as he had been used to do with every moment of leisure, to the old red mill upon the slope. What his offence was he did not know: he sup-posed he had in some manner angered

Baas Cogez by taking the portrait of Alois in the meadow; and when the child who loved him would run to him and nestle her hand in his, he would smile at her very sadly and say with a tender concern for her before himself, "Nay, Alois, do not anger your father. He thinks that I make you idle, dear, and he is not pleased that you should be with me. He is a good man and loves you well: we will not anger him, Alois."

But it was with a sad heart that he said it, and the earth did not look so bright to him as it had used to do when he went out at sunrise under the poplars down the straight roads with Patrasche. The old red mill had been a landmark to him, and he had been used to pause by it, going and coming, for a cheery greeting with its people as her little flaxen head rose above the low mill-wicket, and her little rosy hands had held out a bone or a crust to Patrasche. Now the dog looked wistfully at a closed door, and the boy went on without pausing, with a pang at his heart,

and the child sat within, with tears dropping slowly on the knitting to which she was set, on her little stool by the stove; and Baas Cogez, working among his sacks and his mill-gear, would harden his will and say to himself, "It is best so. The lad is all but a beggar, and full of idle, dreaming fooleries. Who knows what mischief might not come of it in the future?" So he was wise in his generation, and would not have the door unbarred, except upon rare and formal occasions, which seemed to have neither warmth nor mirth in them to the two children, who had been accustomed so long to a daily gleeful, careless, happy interchange of greeting, speech and pastime, with no other watcher of their sports or auditor of their fancies than Patrasche, sagely shaking the brazen bells of his collar and responding with all a dog's swift sympathies to their every change of mood.

All this while the little panel of pine wood remained over the chimney in the mill-kitchen with the cuckoo clock and

the waxen Calvary, and sometimes it seemed to Nello a little hard that whilst his gift was accepted he himself should be denied.

But he did not complain: it was his habit to be quiet: old Jehan Daas had said ever to him, "We are poor: we must take what God sends—the ill with the good: the poor cannot choose."

To which the boy had always listened in silence, being reverent of his old grandfather; but nevertheless a certain vague, sweet hope, such as beguiles the children of genius, had whispered in his heart, "Yet the poor do choose sometimes—choose to be great, so that men cannot say them nay." And he thought so still in his innocence; and one day, when the little Alois, finding him by chance alone amongst the corn-fields by the canal, ran to him and held him close, and sobbed piteously because the morrow would be her saint's day, and for the first time in all her life her parents had failed to bid him to the little supper and romp in the

great barns with which her feast-day was always celebrated. Nello had kissed her and murmured to her in firm faith, "It

shall be different one day, Alois. One day that little bit of pine wood that your father has of mine shall be worth its

weight in silver; and he will not shut the door against me then. Only love me always, dear little Alois, only love me always, and I will be great."

"And if I do not love you?" the pretty child asked, pouting a little through her tears, and moved by the instinctive coquetries of her sex.

Nello's eyes left her face and wandered to the distance, where in the red and gold of the Flemish night the cathedral spire rose. There was a smile on his face so sweet and yet so sad that little Alois was awed by it. "I will be great still," he said under his breath — "great still, or die, Alois."

"You do not love me," said the little spoilt child, pushing him away; but the boy shook his head and smiled, and went on his way through the tall yellow corn, seeing as in a vision some day in a fair future when he should come into that old familiar land and ask Alois of her people, and be not refused or denied, but received in honor, whilst the village folk should

throng to look upon him and say in one another's ears, "Dost see him? He is a king among men, for he is a great artist and the world speaks his name; and yet he was only our poor little Nello, who was a beggar, as one may say, and only got his bread by the help of his dog." And he thought how he would fold his grandsire in furs and purples, and portray him as the old man is portrayed in the Family in the chapel of St. Jacques; and of how he would hang the throat of Patrasche with a collar of gold, and place him on his right hand, and say to the people, "This was once my only friend;" and of how he would build himself a great white marble palace, and make to himself luxuriant gardens of pleasure, on the slope looking outward to where the cathedral spire rose, and not dwell in it himself, but summon to it, as to a home, all men young and poor and friendless, but of the will to do mighty things; and of how he would say to them always, if they sought to bless his name, "Nay, do

not thank me — thank Rubens. Without him, what should I have been?" And these dreams, beautiful, impossible, innocent, free of all selfishness, full of heroical

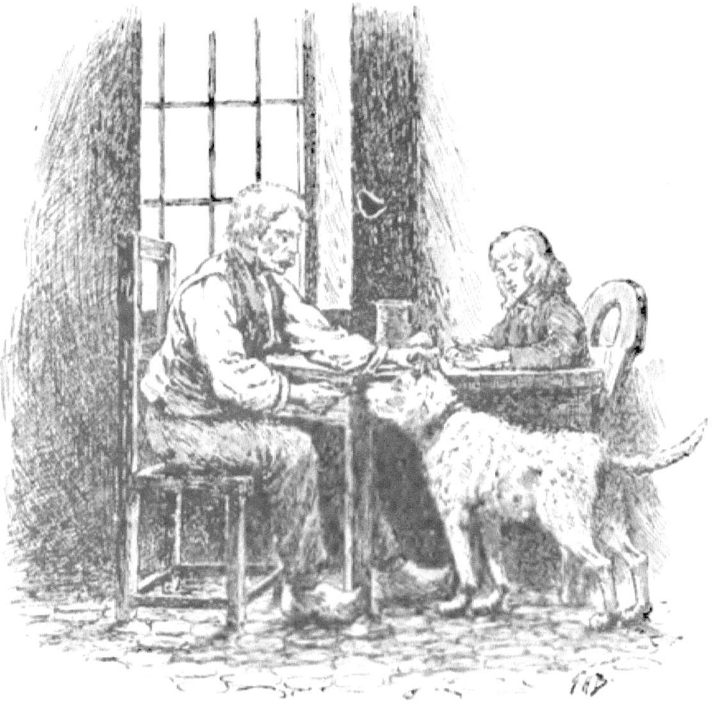

worship, were so closely about him as he went that he was happy — happy even on this sad anniversary of Alois' saint's day, when he and Patrasche went home by themselves to the little dark hut and the

meal of black bread, whilst in the mill-house all the children of the village sang and laughed, and ate the big round cakes of Dijon and the almond gingerbread of Brabant, and danced in the great barn to the light of the stars and the music of flute and fiddle.

"Never mind, Patrasche," he said, with his arms round the dog's neck as they both sat in the door of the hut, where the sounds of the mirth at the mill came down to them on the night air—"never mind. It shall all be changed by and by."

He believed in the future: Patrasche, of more experience and of more philosophy, thought that the loss of the mill supper in the present was ill compensated by dreams of milk and honey in some vague hereafter. And Patrasche growled whenever he passed by Baas Cogez.

"This is Alois' name-day, is it not?" said the old man Daas that night from the corner where he was stretched upon his bed of sacking.

The boy gave a gesture of assent: he wished that the old man's memory had erred a little, instead of keeping such sure account.

"And why not there?" his grandfather pursued. "Thou hast never missed a year before, Nello."

"Thou art too sick to leave," murmured the lad, bending his handsome young head over the bed.

"Tut! tut! Mother Nulette would have come and sat with me, as she does scores of times. What is the cause, Nello?" the old man persisted. "Thou surely hast not had ill words with the little one?"

"Nay, grandfather — never," said the boy quickly, with a hot color in his bent face. "Simply and truly, Baas Cogez did not have me asked this year. He has taken some whim against me."

"But thou hast done nothing wrong?"

"That I know — nothing. I took the portrait of Alois on a piece of pine: that is all."

"Ah!" The old man was silent: the

truth suggested itself to him with the boy's innocent answer. He was tied to a bed of dried leaves in the corner of a wattle hut, but he had not wholly forgotten what the ways of the world were like.

He drew Nello's fair head fondly to his breast with a tenderer gesture. "Thou art very poor, my child," he said with a quiver the more in his aged, trembling voice—"so poor! It is very hard for thee."

"Nay, I am rich," murmured Nello; and in his innocence he thought so—rich with the imperishable powers that are mightier than the might of kings. And he went and stood by the door of the hut in the quiet autumn night, and watched the stars troop by and the tall poplars bend and shiver in the wind. All the casements of the mill-house were lighted, and every now and then the notes of the flute came to him. The tears fell down his cheeks, for he was but a child, yet he smiled, for he said to himself, "In

the future!" He stayed there until all was quite still and dark, then he and Patrasche went within and slept together, long and deeply, side by side.

Now he had a secret which only Patrasche knew. There was a little outhouse to the hut, which no one entered but himself — a dreary place, but with abundant clear light from the north. Here he had fashioned himself rudely an easel in rough lumber, and here, on a great gray sea of stretched paper, he had given shape to one of the innumerable fancies which possessed his brain. No one had ever taught him anything; colors he had no means to buy; he had gone without bread many a time to procure even the few rude vehicles that he had here; and it was only in black or white that he could fashion the things he saw. This great figure which he had drawn here in chalk was only an old man sitting on a fallen tree — only that. He had seen old Michel the woodman sitting so at evening many a time. He had never

had a soul to tell him of outline or perspective, of anatomy or of shadow, and yet he had given all the weary, worn out age, all the sad, quiet patience, all the rugged, careworn pathos of his original, and given them so that the old, lonely figure was a poem, sitting there, meditative and alone, on the dead tree, with the darkness of the descending night behind him.

It was rude, of course, in a way, and had many faults, no doubt; and yet it was real, true in Nature, true in Art, and very mournful, and in a manner beautiful.

Patrasche had lain quiet countless hours watching its gradual creation after the labor of each day was done, and he knew that Nello had a hope — vain and wild, perhaps, but strongly cherished — of sending this great drawing to compete for a prize of two hundred francs a year, which it was announced in Antwerp would be open to every lad of talent, scholar or peasant, under eighteen, who would attempt to win it with some unaided work of chalk or pencil. Three of the fore-

most artists in the town of Rubens were to be the judges and elect the victor according to his merits.

All the spring and summer and autumn Nello had been at work upon this treasure, which, if triumphant, would build him his first step toward independence and the mysteries of the art which he blindly, ignorantly, and yet passionately adored.

He said nothing to any one: his grandfather would not have understood, and little Alois was lost to him. Only to Patrasche he told all, and whispered, "Rubens would give it me, I think, if he knew."

Patrasche thought so too, for he knew that Rubens had loved dogs or he had never painted them with such exquisite fidelity; and men who loved dogs were, as Patrasche knew, always pitiful.

The drawings were to go in on the first day of December, and the decision be given

on the twenty-fourth, so that he who should win might rejoice with all his people at the Christmas season.

In the twilight of a bitter wintry day, and with a beating heart, now quick with hope, now faint with fear, Nello placed the great picture on his little, green milk-cart, and took it, with the help of Patrasche, into the town, and there left it, as enjoined, at the doors of a public building.

"Perhaps it is worth nothing at all. How can I tell?" he thought, with the heart-sickness of a great timidity. Now that he had left it there, it seemed to him so hazardous, so vain, so foolish, to dream that he, a little lad with bare feet, who barely knew his letters, could do anything at which great painters, real artists, could ever deign to look. Yet he took heart as he went by the cathedral: the lordly form of Rubens seemed to rise from the fog and the darkness, and to loom in its magnificence before him, whilst the lips, with their kindly smile, seemed to him to murmur, "Nay, have courage! It was not by a weak

heart and by faint fears that I wrote my name for all time upon Antwerp."

Nello ran home through the cold night, comforted. He had done his best: the rest must be as God willed, he thought, in that innocent, unquestioning faith which had been taught him in the little gray chapel amongst the willows and the poplar trees.

The winter was very sharp already. That night, after they reached the hut, snow fell; and fell for very many days after that, so that the paths and the divisions in the fields were all obliterated, and all the smaller streams were frozen over, and the cold was intense upon the plains. Then, indeed, it became hard work to go round for the milk while the world was all dark, and carry it through the darkness to the silent town. Hard work, especially for Patrasche, for the passage of the years, that were only bringing Nello a stronger youth, were bringing him old age, and his joints were stiff, and his bones ached often. But he would never give up his share of

the labor. Nello would fain have spared him and drawn the cart himself, but Patrasche would not allow it. All he would ever permit or accept was the help of a thrust from behind to the truck, as it lumbered along through the ice-ruts. Patrasche had lived in harness, and he was proud of it. He suffered a great deal sometimes from frost, and the terrible roads, and the rheumatic pains of his limbs, but he only drew his breath hard and bent his stout neck, and trod onward with steady patience.

"Rest thee at home, Patrasche — it is time thou didst rest — and I can quite well push in the cart by myself," urged Nello many a morning; but Patrasche, who understood him aright, would no more have consented to stay at home than a veteran soldier to shirk when the charge was sounding; and every day he would rise and place himself in his shafts, and plod along over the snow through the fields that his four round feet had left their print upon so many, many years.

"One must never rest till one dies," thought Patrasche; and sometimes it seemed to him that that time of rest for him was not very far off. His sight was less clear than it had been, and it gave him pain to rise after the night's sleep, though he would never lie a moment in his straw when once the bell of the chapel tolling five let him know that the daybreak of labor had begun.

"My poor Patrasche, we shall soon lie quiet together, you and I," said old Jehan Daas, stretching out to stroke the head of Patrasche with the old, withered hand which had always shared with him its one poor crust of bread; and the hearts of the old man and the old dog ached together with one thought: When they were gone, who would care for their darling?

One afternoon, as they came back from Antwerp over the snow, which had become hard and smooth as marble over all the Flemish plains, they found dropped in the road a pretty little puppet, a tambourine-player, all scarlet and gold, about six

inches high, and, unlike greater personages when Fortune lets them drop, quite unspoiled and unhurt by its fall. It was a pretty toy. Nello tried to find its owner,

and, failing, thought that it was just the thing to please Alois.

It was quite night when he passed the mill-house: he knew the little window of her room. It could be no harm, he

thought, if he gave her his little piece of treasure-trove, they had been play-fellows so long. There was a shed with a sloping roof beneath her casement: he climbed it and tapped softly at the lattice: there was a little light within. The child opened it and looked out, half frightened.

Nello put the tambourine-player into her hands. "Here is a doll I found in the snow, Alois. Take it," he whispered—"take it, and God bless thee, dear!"

He slid down from the shed-roof before she had time to thank him, and ran off through the darkness.

That night there was a fire at the mill. Out-buildings and much corn were destroyed, although the mill itself and the dwelling-house were unharmed. All the village was out in terror, and engines came tearing through the snow from Antwerp. The miller was insured, and would lose nothing: nevertheless, he was in furious wrath, and declared aloud that the fire was due to no accident, but to some foul intent.

Nello, awakened from his sleep, ran to help with the rest: Baas Cogez thrust him angrily aside. "Thou wert loitering here after dark," he said roughly. "I believe, on my soul, that thou dost know more of the fire than any one."

Nello heard him in silence, stupefied, not supposing that any one could say such things except in jest, and not comprehending how any one could pass a jest at such a time.

Nevertheless, the miller said the brutal thing openly to many of his neighbors in the day that followed; and though no serious charge was ever preferred against the lad, it got bruited about that Nello had been seen in the mill-yard after dark on some unspoken errand, and that he bore Baas Cogez a grudge for forbidding his intercourse with little Alois; and so the hamlet, which followed the sayings of its richest landowner servilely, and whose families all hoped to secure the riches of Alois in some future time for their sons, took the hint to give grave looks and cold

words to old Jehan Daas' grandson. No one said anything to him openly, but all the village agreed together to humor the miller's prejudice, and at the cottages and farms where Nello and Patrasche called every morning for the milk for Antwerp, downcast glances and brief phrases replaced to them the broad smiles and cheerful greetings to which they had been always used. No one really credited the miller's absurd suspicion, nor the outrageous accusations born of them, but the people were all very poor and very ignorant, and the one rich man of the place had pronounced against him. Nello, in his innocence and his friendlessness, had no strength to stem the popular tide.

"Thou art very cruel to the lad," the miller's wife dared to say, weeping, to her lord. "Sure he is an innocent lad and a faithful, and would never dream of any such wickedness, however sore his heart might be."

But Baas Cogez being an obstinate man, having once said a thing held to it dog-

gedly, though in his innermost soul he knew well the injustice that he was committing.

Meanwhile, Nello endured the injury done against him with a certain proud patience that disdained to complain: he only gave way a little when he was quite alone with old Patrasche. Besides, he thought, "If it should win! They will be sorry then, perhaps."

Still, to a boy not quite sixteen, and who had dwelt in one little world all his short life, and in his childhood had been caressed and applauded on all sides, it was a hard trial to have the whole of that little world turn against him for naught. Especially hard in that bleak, snow-bound, famine-stricken winter-time, when the only light and warmth there could be found abode beside the village hearths and in the kindly greetings of neighbors. In the winter-time all drew nearer to each other, all to all, except to Nello and Patrasche, with whom none now would have anything to do, and who

were left to fare as they might with the old paralyzed, bedridden man in the little cabin, whose fire was often low, and whose board was often without bread, for there was a buyer from Antwerp who had taken to drive his mule in of a day for the milk of the various dairies, and there were only three or four of the people who had refused his terms of purchase and remained faithful to the little green cart. So that the burden which Patrasche drew had become very light, and the centime-pieces in Nello's pouch had become, alas! very small likewise.

The dog would stop, as usual, at all the familiar gates which were now closed to him, and look up at them with wistful, mute appeal; and it cost the neighbors a pang to shut their doors and their hearts, and let Patrasche draw his cart on again, empty. Nevertheless, they did it, for they desired to please Baas Cogez.

Noël was close at hand.

The weather was very wild and cold. The snow was six feet deep, and the ice

was firm enough to bear oxen and men upon it everywhere. At this season the little village was always gay and cheerful. At the poorest dwelling there were possets and cakes, joking and dancing, sugared saints and gilded Jésus. The merry Flemish bells jingled everywhere on the horses; everywhere within doors some well-filled soup-pot sang and smoked over the stove; and everywhere over the snow without laughing maidens pattered in bright kerchiefs and stout kirtles, going to and from the mass. Only in the little hut it was very dark and very cold.

Nello and Patrasche were left utterly alone, for one night in the week before the Christmas Day, Death entered there, and took away from life for ever old Jehan Daas, who had never known of life aught save its poverty and its pains. He had long been half dead, incapable of any movement except a feeble gesture, and powerless for anything beyond a gentle word; and yet his loss fell on them both with a great horror in it: they mourned

him passionately. He had passed away from them in his sleep, and when in the gray dawn they learned their bereavement, unutterable solitude and desolation seemed

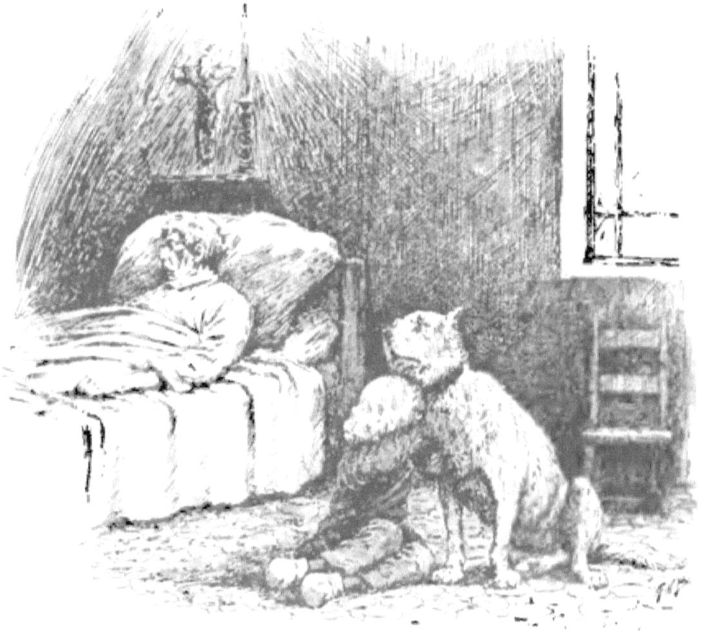

to close around them. He had long been only a poor, feeble, paralyzed old man, who could not raise a hand in their defence, but he had loved them well: his smile had always welcomed their return. They mourned for him unceasingly, refus-

ing to be comforted, as in the white winter day they followed the deal shell that held his body to the nameless grave by the little gray church. They were his only mourners, these two whom he had left friendless upon earth — the young boy and the old dog. "Surely, he will relent now and let the poor lad come hither?" thought the miller's wife, glancing at her husband where he smoked by the hearth.

Baas Cogez knew her thought, but he hardened his heart, and would not unbar his door as the little, humble funeral went by. "The boy is a beggar," he said to himself: "he shall not be about Alois."

The woman dared not say anything aloud, but when the grave was closed and the mourners had gone, she put a wreath of immortelles into Alois' hands and bade her go and lay it reverently on the dark, unmarked mound where the snow was displaced.

Nello and Patrasche went home with

broken hearts. But even of that poor, melancholy, cheerless home they were denied the consolation. There was a month's rent over-due for their little home, and when Nello had paid the last sad service to the dead he had not a coin left. He went and begged grace of the owner of the hut, a cobbler who went every Sunday night to drink his pint of wine and smoke with Baas Cogez. The cobbler would grant no mercy. He was a harsh, miserly man, and loved money. He claimed in default of his rent every stick and stone, every pot and pan, in the hut, and bade Nello and Patrasche be out of it on the morrow.

Now, the cabin was lowly enough, and in some sense miserable enough, and yet their hearts clove to it with a great affection. They had been so happy there, and in the summer, with its clambering vine and its flowering beans, it was so pretty and bright in the midst of the sun-lighted fields! Their life in it had been full of labor and privation, and yet they had been

so well content, so gay of heart, running together to meet the old man's never-failing smile of welcome!

All night long the boy and the dog sat by the fireless hearth in the darkness, drawn close together for warmth and sorrow. Their bodies were insensible to the cold, but their hearts seemed frozen in them.

When the morning broke over the white, chill earth it was the morning of Christmas Eve. With a shudder, Nello clasped close to him his only friend, while his tears fell hot and fast on the dog's frank forehead. "Let us go, Patrasche — dear, dear Patrasche," he murmured. "We will not wait to be kicked out: let us go."

Patrasche had no will but his, and they went sadly, side by side, out from the little place which was so dear to them both, and in which every humble, homely thing was to them precious and beloved. Patrasche drooped his head wearily as he passed by his own green cart: it was no longer his

—it had to go with the rest to pay the rent, and his brass harness lay idle and glittering on the snow. The dog could have lain down beside it and died for very heart-sickness as he went, but whilst the lad lived and needed him Patrasche would not yield and give way.

They took the old accustomed road into Antwerp. The day had yet scarce more than dawned, most of the shutters were still closed, but some of the villagers were about. They took no notice whilst the dog and the boy passed by them. At one door Nello paused and looked wistfully within: his grandfather had done many a kindly turn in neighbor's service to the people who dwelt there.

"Would you give Patrasche a crust?" he said, timidly. "He is old, and he has had nothing since last forenoon."

The woman shut the door hastily, murmuring some vague saying about wheat and rye being very dear that season. The boy and the dog went on again wearily: they asked no more.

By slow and painful ways they reached Antwerp as the chimes tolled ten.

"If I had anything about me I could sell to get him bread!" thought Nello, but he had nothing except the wisp of

linen and serge that covered him, and his pair of wooden shoes.

Patrasche understood, and nestled his nose into the lad's hand, as though to pray him not to be disquieted for any woe or want of his.

The winner of the drawing-prize was to be proclaimed at noon, and to the pub-

lic building where he had left his treasure Nello made his way. On the steps and in the entrance-hall there was a crowd of youths — some of his age, some older, all with parents or relatives or friends. His heart was sick with fear as he went amongst them, holding Patrasche close to him. The great bells of the city clashed out the hour of noon with brazen clamor. The doors of the inner hall were opened; the eager, panting throng rushed in: it was known that the selected picture would be raised above the rest upon a wooden dais.

A mist obscured Nello's sight, his head swam, his limbs almost failed him. When his vision cleared he saw the drawing raised on high: it was not his own! A slow, sonorous voice was proclaiming aloud that victory had been adjudged to Stephan Kiesslinger, born in the burgh of Antwerp, son of a wharfinger in that town.

When Nello recovered his consciousness he was lying on the stones without,

and Patrasche was trying with every art he knew to call him back to life. In the distance a throng of the youths of Antwerp were shouting around their successful comrade, and escorting him with acclamations to his home upon the quay.

The boy staggered to his feet and drew the dog into his embrace. "It is all over, dear Patrasche," he murmured—"all over!"

He rallied himself as best he could, for he was weak from fasting, and retraced his steps to the village. Patrasche paced by his side with his head drooping and his old limbs feeble from hunger and sorrow.

The snow was falling fast: a keen hurricane blew from the north: it was bitter as death on the plains. It took them long to traverse the familiar path, and the bells were sounding four of the clock as they approached the hamlet. Suddenly Patrasche paused, arrested by a scent in the snow, scratched, whined, and drew out with his teeth a small case of brown

leather. He held it up to Nello in the darkness. Where they were there stood a little Calvary, and a lamp burned dully under the cross: the boy mechanically turned the case to the light: on it was the name of Baas Cogez, and within it were notes for two thousand francs.

The sight roused the lad a little from his stupor. He thrust it in his shirt, and stroked Patrasche and drew him onward. The dog looked up wistfully in his face.

Nello made straight for the mill-house, and went to the house-door and struck on its panels. The miller's wife opened it weeping, with little Alois cling-

ing close to her skirts. "Is it thee, thou poor lad?" she said kindly through her tears. "Get thee gone ere the Baas see thee. We are in sore trouble to-night. He is out seeking for a power of money that he has let fall riding homeward, and in this snow he never will find it; and God knows it will go nigh to ruin us. It is Heaven's own judgment for the things we have done to thee."

Nello put the note-case in her hand and called Patrasche within the house. "Patrasche found the money to-night," he said quickly. "Tell Baas Cogez so: I think he will not deny the dog shelter and food in his old age. Keep him from pursuing me, and I pray of you to be good to him."

Ere either woman or dog knew what he meant he had stooped and kissed Patrasche: then closed the door hurriedly, and disappeared in the gloom of the fast-falling night.

The woman and the child stood speechless with joy and fear: Patrasche vainly

spent the fury of his anguish against the iron-bound oak of the barred house-door. They did not dare unbar the door and let him forth: they tried all they could to solace him. They brought him sweet cakes and juicy meats; they tempted him with the best they had; they tried to lure him to abide by the warmth of the hearth; but it was of no avail. Patrasche refused to be comforted or to stir from the barred portal.

It was six o'clock when from an opposite entrance the miller at last came, jaded and broken, into his wife's presence. "It is lost for ever," he said with an ashen cheek and a quiver in his stern voice. "We have looked with lanterns everywhere: it is gone — the little maiden's portion and all!"

His wife put the money into his hand, and told him how it had come to her. The strong man sank trembling into a seat and covered his face, ashamed and almost afraid. "I have been cruel to the lad," he muttered at length: "I deserved not to have good at his hands."

Little Alois, taking courage, crept close to her father and nestled against him her fair curly head. "Nello may come here again, father?" she whispered. "He may come to-morrow as he used to do?"

The miller pressed her in his arms: his hard, sun-burned face was very pale and his mouth trembled. "Surely, surely," he answered his child. "He shall bide here on Christmas Day, and any other day he will. God helping me, I will make amends to the boy — I will make amends."

Little Alois kissed him in gratitude and joy, then slid from his knees and ran to where the dog kept watch by the door. "And to-night I may feast Patrasche?" she cried in a child's thoughtless glee.

Her father bent his head gravely: "Ay, ay: let the dog have the best;" for the stern old man was moved and shaken to his heart's depths.

It was Christmas Eve, and the mill-house was filled with oak logs and squares of turf, with cream and honey, with meat

and bread, and the rafters were hung with wreaths of evergreen, and the Calvary and the cuckoo clock looked out from a mass of holly. There were little paper lanterns too for Alois, and toys of various fashions and sweetmeats in bright-pictured papers. There were light and warmth and abundance everywhere, and the child would fain have made the dog a guest honored and feasted.

But Patrasche would neither lie in the warmth nor share in the cheer. Famished he was, and very cold, but without Nello he would partake neither of comfort nor food. Against all temptation he was proof, and close against the door he leaned always, watching only for a means of escape.

"He wants the lad," said Baas Cogez. "Good dog! good dog! I will go over to the lad the first thing at day-dawn." For no one but Patrasche knew that Nello had left the

hut, and no one but Patrasche divined that Nello had gone to face starvation and misery alone.

The mill-kitchen was very warm; great logs crackled and flamed on the hearth;

neighbors came in for a glass of wine and a slice of the fat goose baking for supper. Alois, gleeful and sure of her playmate back on the morrow, bounded and sang and tossed back her yellow hair. Baas Cogez, in the fulness of his heart, smiled on her through moistened eyes, and spoke

of the way in which he would befriend her favorite companion; the house-mother sat with calm, contented face at the spinning-wheel; the cuckoo in the clock chirped mirthful hours. Amidst it all Patrasche was bidden with a thousand words of welcome to tarry there a cherished guest. But neither peace nor plenty could allure him where Nello was not.

When the supper smoked on the board, and the voices were loudest and gladdest, and the Christ-child brought choicest gifts to Alois, Patrasche, watching always an occasion, glided out when the door was unlatched by a careless new-comer, and as swiftly as his weak and tired limbs would bear him sped over the snow in the bitter, black night. He had only one thought — to follow Nello. A human friend might have paused for the pleasant meal, the cherry warmth, the cozy slumber; but that was not the friendship of Patrasche. He remembered a bygone time, when an old man and a little child had found him sick unto death in the wayside ditch.

Snow had fallen freshly all the evening long; it was now nearly ten; the trail of the boy's footsteps was almost obliterated. It took Patrasche long to discover any scent. When at last he found it, it was lost again quickly, and lost and recovered, and again lost and again recovered, a hundred times or more.

The night was very wild. The lamps under the wayside crosses were blown out; the roads were sheets of ice; the impenetrable darkness hid every trace of habitations; there was no living thing abroad. All the cattle were housed, and in all the huts and homesteads men and women rejoiced and feasted. There was only Patrasche out in the cruel cold — old and famished and full of pain, but with the strength and the patience of a great love to sustain him in his search.

The trail of Nello's steps, faint and ob-

scure as it was under the new snow, went straightly along the accustomed tracks into Antwerp. It was past midnight when Patrasche traced it over the boundaries of the town and into the narrow, tortuous, gloomy streets. It was all quite dark in the town, save where some light gleamed

ruddily through the crevices of house-shutters, or some group went homeward with lanterns chanting drinking-songs. The streets were all white with ice: the high walls and roofs loomed black against them. There was scarce a sound save the riot of the winds down the passages as they tossed the creaking signs and shook the tall lamp-irons.

So many passers-by had trodden through and through the snow, so many diverse paths had crossed and recrossed each other, that the dog had a hard task to retain any hold on the track he followed. But he kept on his way, though the cold

pierced him to the bone, and the jagged ice cut his feet, and the hunger in his body gnawed like a rat's teeth. He kept on his way, a poor, gaunt, shivering thing,

and by long patience traced the steps he loved into the very heart of the burgh and up to the steps of the great cathedral.

"He is gone to the things that he loved," thought Patrasche: he could not

understand, but he was full of sorrow and of pity for the art-passion that to him was so incomprehensible and yet so sacred.

The portals of the cathedral were unclosed after the midnight mass. Some heedlessness in the custodians, too eager to go home and feast or sleep, or too drowsy to know whether they turned the keys aright, had left one of the doors unlocked. By that accident the footfalls Patrasche sought had passed through into the building, leaving the white marks of snow upon the dark stone floor. By that slender white thread, frozen as it fell, he was guided through the intense silence, through the immensity of the vaulted space — guided straight to the gates of the chancel, and, stretched there upon the stones, he found Nello. He crept up and touched the face of the boy. "Didst thou dream that I should be faithless and forsake thee? I, — a dog?" said that mute caress.

The lad raised himself with a low cry and clasped him close. "Let us lie down

and die together," he murmured. "Men have no need of us, and we are all alone."

In answer, Patrasche crept closer yet, and laid his head upon the young boy's breast. The great tears stood in his brown, sad eyes: not for himself — for himself he was happy.

They lay close together in the piercing cold. The blasts that blew over the Flemish dikes from the northern seas were like waves of ice, which froze every living thing they touched. The interior of the immense vault of stone in which they were was even more bitterly chill than the snow-covered plains without. Now and then a bat moved in the shadows — now and then a gleam of light came on the ranks of carven figures. Under the Rubens they lay together quite still, and soothed almost into a dreaming slumber by the numbing narcotic of the cold. Together they dreamed of the old glad days when they had chased each other through the flowering grasses of the summer meadows, or sat hidden in the tall bulrushes by the water's

side, watching the boats go seaward in the sun.

Suddenly through the darkness a great white radiance streamed through the vastness of the aisles; the moon, that was at

her height, had broken through the clouds, the snow had ceased to fall, the light reflected from the snow without was clear as the light of dawn. It fell through the arches full upon the two pictures above, from which the boy on his entrance had flung back the veil: the Elevation and the Descent of the Cross were for one instant visible.

Nello rose to his feet and stretched his arms to them: the tears of a passionate ecstasy glistened on the paleness of his face. "I have seen them at last!" he cried aloud. "O God, it is enough!"

His limbs failed under him, and he sank upon his knees, still gazing upward at the

majesty that he adored. For a few brief moments the light illumined the divine visions that had been denied to him so long — light clear and sweet and strong as though it streamed from the throne of Heaven. Then suddenly it passed away: once more a great darkness covered the face of Christ.

The arms of the boy drew close again the body of the dog. "We shall see His face — *there*," he murmured; "and He will not part us, I think."

On the morrow, by the chancel of the cathedral, the people of Antwerp found them both. They were both dead: the cold of the night had frozen into stillness alike the young life and the old. When the Christmas morning broke and the priests came to the temple, they saw them lying thus on the stones together. Above, the veils were drawn back from the great visions of Rubens, and the fresh rays of the sunrise touched the thorn-crowned head of the Christ.

As the day grew on there came an old,

hard-featured man who wept as women weep. "I was cruel to the lad," he muttered, "and now I would have made amends — yea, to the half of my substance — and he should have been to me as a son."

There came also, as the day grew apace, a painter who had fame in the world, and who was liberal of hand and of spirit. "I seek one who should have had the prize yesterday had worth won," he said to the people — "a boy of rare promise and genius. An old wood-cutter on a fallen tree at eventide — that was all his theme. But there was greatness for the future in it. I would fain find him, and take him with me and teach him Art."

And a little child with curling fair hair, sobbing bitterly as she clung to her father's arm, cried aloud, "Oh, Nello, come! We have all ready for thee. The Christ-child's hands are full of gifts, and the old piper will play for us; and the mother says thou shalt stay by the hearth and burn nuts with us all the Noël week long — yes,

even to the Feast of the Kings! And Patrasche will be so happy! Oh, Nello, wake and come!"

But the young pale face, turned upward to the light of the great Rubens with a smile upon its mouth, answered them all, "It is too late."

For the sweet, sonorous bells went ringing through the frost, and the sunlight shone upon the plains of snow, and the populace trooped gay and glad through the streets, but Nello and Patrasche no more asked charity at their hands. All they needed now Antwerp gave unbidden.

Death had been more pitiful to them than longer life would have been. It had taken the one in the loyalty of love, and the other in the innocence of faith, from a world which for love has no recompense and for faith no fulfilment.

All their lives they had been together, and in their deaths they were not divided; for when they were found the arms of the boy were folded too closely around the dog to be severed without violence, and

the people of their little village, contrite and ashamed, implored a special grace for them, and, making them one grave, laid them to rest there side by side — for ever!

www.ingramcontent.com/pod-product-compliance
Lightning Source LLC
Chambersburg PA
CBHW020808020726
47495CB00008B/2634
* 9 7 8 3 7 4 3 4 2 7 6 9 3 *

www.ingramcontent.com/pod-product-compliance
Lightning Source LLC
Chambersburg PA
CBHW020753020726
47495CB00008B/2408